The eart
just the

"It's the tsuna...
Tansy. "We h...
They sweep right across the islands,
destroying everything in their path."

Grimly, Blake took her hand and led the
way back to the jeep and Tansy
thankfully clung to the side to keep
from bouncing out as Blake drove
madly toward higher ground. But a
dislodged boulder came crashing down
onto the radiator.

"We'll have to run for it." Blake pulled
her up the mountain path after him but
the roaring, rushing sound of water in
the distance grew ever louder and Tansy
knew with a horrifying certainty they
weren't going to make it....

# OTHER
# *Harlequin Romances*
## by SALLY WENTWORTH

# Conflict in Paradise

by

## SALLY WENTWORTH

*Harlequin Books*

TORONTO • LONDON • NEW YORK • AMSTERDAM
SYDNEY • HAMBURG • PARIS

Original hardcover edition published in 1978
by Mills & Boon Limited

ISBN 0-373-02207-7

Harlequin edition published October 1978

PRINTED IN U.S.A.

# CHAPTER ONE

THE muscles of the four native rowers rippled beneath their bronzed skins as they sent the wooden outrigger canoe racing across the ocean, their paddles leaving a swirl of phosphorescence in the boat's wake. Above their heads the white, triangular sail took advantage of every puff of breeze to send them scudding towards Aparoa, the small Pacific island that had been home to Tansy Harland for as long as she could remember. Ordinarily she would have enjoyed the voyage, would have been absorbed in watching the skill of the men as they avoided the dangerous coral heads that lay just beneath the surface, or in looking out for the sea creatures visible from her seat almost level with the water; sea turtles that swam hastily away at their swift approach, shoals of brilliantly coloured fish, and often the dark fin of a basking shark that would come curiously up to them and then go off to look for easier prey. Once or twice Tansy had been lucky enough to sight a whale, but that had been many years ago, before man had hunted them in such numbers that they were now virtually extinct. Just as men were now coming to her beloved island and threatening to tear it apart! Tansy thought grimly.

The news that Aparoa was being considered as a site for a refuelling base for a combined NATO force in the South Pacific had come as a bombshell only a few weeks ago. Tansy had been quietly eating breakfast on the veranda of their house, one of the few two-storied buildings on the island, while her father, Dr David Harland, had been listening out on the radio transmitter in the remote chance that any of the news items might possibly affect the island, when the operator gave their call sign. Dr Harland had taken the message down and acknowledged it without really taking in its full import. Rather dazedly he held the notepad out for Tansy to look at. Quickly she read his sprawling writing and then stared at her father with equal incredulity.

'But there must be some mistake. They can't possibly mean Aparoa,' she said in astonishment. 'The lagoon isn't deep enough to take big boats any more, and there isn't anywhere for a plane to land. Are you quite sure it was meant for us, Daddy?'

'Quite sure, my dear. The operator repeated our call sign twice.' Dr Harland re-read the message with a worried frown on his face. 'They ask me to give every assistance to the army survey team that will be coming here to report on the suitability of the island,' he murmured. 'You know, Tansy, I don't like the look of this. We certainly don't want a fuel base built here if we can possibly avoid it. I'd better go and have a word with Tupuhoe and Ruari; see what they think about it. Will you take the clinic this morning, my dear?'

'Yes, of course.' While her father had gone off to the headman's house to acquaint him and his son, Ruari, with the news, Tansy had collected her medical bag and made her way uneasily to the small clinic in the nearby village that fringed the sea shore. She tried to tell herself that the whole thing was quite ridiculous; that Aparoa was entirely unsuitable for the government's purpose, and that the survey team would take one look at the island and go elsewhere, but somehow she couldn't shake off the nagging doubts at the back of her mind. Her patients were unused to seeing her without her bright smile and started asking curious questions; having known her since early childhood they felt no more reticence in questioning her than they would have felt towards any other islander. Besides, they were like children in their avid curiosity and liked to know everything about their neighbours' business.

Tansy pulled herself together and laughingly parried their questions, but was just as eager in putting her own when her father at length returned from Tupuhoe's house with Ruari at his side. Ruari smiled reassuringly at Tansy as, the last of the patients gone, they returned to the doctor's house and sat round the table on the veranda with a fruit juice for Tansy and bottles of beer for the men.

'My father, too, is greatly worried by this piece of news,' he told her. 'It will be a very bad thing for the island if they build a fuelling station here.' Ruari spoke English with a slight Australian accent, being one of the few islanders who had been educated in that country. Of the others, some were still completing their education, but two had chosen not to return to the narrow confines of Aparoa, a fact which had greatly saddened the chief and David Harland, who had himself contributed quite a large part of his government salary to help send the children to school.

'Is there nothing we can do to prevent it?' Tansy asked them.

'We've been talking about that,' her father told her. 'We think that perhaps the best thing would be for me to go to Australia myself and find out exactly what's going on, and see if I can't pull a few strings to make absolutely sure that they don't use Aparoa as a base. Not that it's at all likely,' he added optimistically, 'but it's just as

well to point out to these government bods just how mad
they are to even contemplate it.'

So Dr Harland had gone to Australia on the next
inter-island schooner, a decision which greatly under-
lined his own misgivings, for he left the island as seldom
as possible, and Tansy, herself a fully qualified doctor,
had been left to take care of the sick on Aparoa and on
the many scattered volcanic or coral islands in the vicin-
ity, the more outlying of which took two to three days
to reach by sailing canoe, stopping at night at the nearest
convenient island. Tansy had been visiting one of these
when she received word by radio from Ruari that the
survey team had arrived, despite all her father's efforts
to prevent it in the short time he had been in Australia.

Now the high central mountain of Aparoa, forced up
out of the sea long ago by volcanic action, appeared on
the edge of their limited horizon, and, as if the sight of
their home had given them added strength, the men sent
the paddles dipping even faster into the sea. Soon the
tops of the coconut palms that stretched for over a mile
inland came into sight and Tansy could make out the
high grey walls of the old prison buildings on the west
side of the bay, just below the head of the long plateau
where the palm trees grew.

Skilfully the natives steered the canoe through the gap
in the outer coral reef, kept open by the surge of fresh
water that flowed from the river mouth, across the
lagoon and into the open sea. As coral cannot live in
fresh water this channel was one of the few places where
a boat could always approach the island in safety. The
army boat, too, had come this way, for Tansy could see
it moored at the crumbling old stone jetty below the
prison; a powerful, shallow-drafted vessel, purpose-built
for negotiating this kind of island. Tansy looked at it

longingly, thinking how quickly she could answer an emergency call if she had such a boat at her disposal. Admittedly they had had a motor-boat once, but it had broken down and, although Ruari knew quite a bit about engines and could have repaired it, the government suppliers had sent the wrong parts, and then sent the right parts to the wrong group of islands. They were probably now lost deep in the hold of some island schooner being ferried continuously about the South Pacific, despite David Harland's urgent messages asking for replacements. It seemed priority was given to men of war rather than men of peace, Tansy thought bitterly as she gazed across at the graceful vessel.

The shore came up to meet them now, a strip of white sand slipping into blue water, and then Tansy was jumping out of the canoe to wade the few steps to the beach. Immediately she was surrounded by a group of eager children until she picked one bright-eyed child to carry her medical bag up to the house. This was deemed a great honour and the bag was carried with extreme care and self-importance, rather as if it was some kind of idol; often Tansy thought that the islanders, although all devout Christians, still showed some traces of their old pagan ancestry in the way they looked upon the 'magical' cures that came out of her medical bag.

Several adults had also come to meet her; they talked softly in their lilting Polynesian tongue, telling her of the soldiers' arrival, that they had taken possession of the old prison. These grim, fortresslike buildings had originally been built as a convict colony in the days when British prisoners, who were too dangerous to be transported to Australia, had been sent to Aparoa instead, but they had stood empty now for over a hundred years. As Tansy looked towards them she saw a jeep emerge and drive down towards the jetty where, despite the gathering dusk, supplies were still being unloaded from the boat. The noise of the jeep's engine made a harsh, alien sound on the island, for there were no motor vehicles on Aparoa, only horses and bicycles to get about on.

An officer, tall in tropical kit, got out of the jeep and looked across to where the natives were still gathered round her. He hesitated, as if about to come across the beach to them, and Tansy hastily drew back among the others; she had no wish to speak to the soldiers until she had learnt what she could of them from Ruari. Then she realised how senseless it was to try to conceal herself; her long blonde hair, bleached to platinum by the sun, made her stand out like a beacon from the dark-haired Aparoans around her. But one of the soldiers must have asked the officer a question, for he turned back and Tansy was able to hurry along the road to the village and Ruari's house.

News of her arrival had, as always, travelled ahead of her and she had not gone very far before she saw Ruari coming to meet her. Like all the male islanders, he wore European clothing, but where most of the others wore loose-fitting cotton trousers and shirts, Ruari had progressed to denim jeans and a tee-shirt that failed to hide the strong shoulder muscles gained from years of diving for mother-of-pearl mussels and trochus shells. He was twenty-seven years old, a handsome young man who was working hard to bring all the benefits of progress to Aparoa without any of its disadvantages, an aim in which Tansy sincerely believed and gave her wholehearted support. Among the single girls Ruari was considered a great catch, but as yet he had shown no preference for any particular maiden. Having been brought up and encouraged to look upon him almost as a brother, Tansy was always on completely easy terms with him.

'Have you spoken to the soldiers yet? How long do they intend to stay? Have you managed to contact Daddy and tell him?' Anxiously Tansy questioned him before he had even had time to greet her.

Ruari held up his hands in laughing protest. 'One question at a time, and I'll take the last one first. Yes, I've talked to your father over the radio and he's managed to get in touch with some old friends who may be able to help. He'll be away for another few days following up that lead, but he advised us not to worry too much; it seems that survey teams are also looking at two other islands and no definite choice has been made yet. Now, what were your other questions? Oh, yes. We don't know how long they will stay, probably only a week or so, I expect; and no, I haven't spoken to them. No one has.'

He emphasised the last sentence and Tansy grinned back at him delightedly. It was an old ploy of the islanders towards unwelcome strangers to pretend that they couldn't understand English, although most of them spoke a fair amount of the language, and all of them spoke excellent Pidgin and some French as well as their native Polynesian.

Ruari's teeth gleamed in his brown face as he continued, 'First of all the officer, a Major Aston, tried to find your father but failed to do so, of course, then he came to my house and tried to talk to *my* father, but Tupuhoe can be very deaf when he wants to be, especially when he isn't wearing that hearing aid that Dr Harland obtained from Australia for him.'

Tansy gurgled with laughter. 'He must have been furious! Then what happened?' she asked eagerly.

'Then he went to the prison and found it all locked up. Old Amaru has the key, of course, and won't give it up to anyone because she keeps her pigs in the court-yard there where no one will steal them. Well, by now the whole village had gathered round and, as the walls are too high and steep to climb, the officer had the lock broken open. Immediately the gates were opened the pigs came squealing out and everyone started trying to catch them, the soldiers too. Then Amaru started scream-ing that the soldiers were trying to steal her pigs and all the villagers joined in the melée until the whole place was a riot of squealing pigs and shouting people.'

He stopped for breath and Tansy wiped tears of laughter from her eyes. 'Oh, how I wish I'd been there to see it! But how did it end?'

Ruari's face sobered and he became serious. 'The officer stopped it. He simply fired his pistol in the air. Everyone was immediately shocked into silence and then he gave several biting orders and, how I don't quite know, suddenly everything had sorted itself out. We were moved out of the way, the soldiers began to take their equipment in, and the children were sent off to round up the pigs. Even old Amaru was quiet for once.' He looked at Tansy. 'The officer is a professional, Tansy. It may not be so easy to convince him that Aparoa is un-suitable for a base.'

'Nonsense,' she returned determinedly. 'We just have to play for time, that's all. If Daddy is successful with these friends of his the soldiers will probably be re-called in a few days anyway, but in the meantime it won't do any harm to let the army see just how little co-operation they're going to get from us.'

They talked a little longer, but soon Tansy left him to go to her own house. She had lived here for over twenty years, ever since her father had brought her to Aparoa as a toddler, and she loved the old house, its mellowed stone walls almost hidden beneath climbing plants that were ablaze with colour. For a moment Tansy paused on the veranda to look out to sea to the sunset that spread itself like a peacock's tail, iridescent and brilliant, across the horizon. How peaceful and lovely the island was, set like a jewel in the ocean; silently she prayed that its peace would not be destroyed by the orders of men in faraway government offices, who could never have even contemplated such desecration if they had seen this beauty for themselves.

Sighing, Tansy went indoors, turning on one of the lamps in the big living room before sitting down to the meal that Inara, their servant girl, had left out for her. Then she went to have a bath, the water for which flowed from a water tank on the roof, but she was still rinsing her hair when she heard a loud knocking at the front door. Thinking that it must be one of the islanders in need of medical help, she called out in Polynesian, asking them to wait, while she wrapped a sarong round her still wet body and put a towel over her hair, turban fashion, completely covering it.

The peremptory knocking came again and Tansy started to remonstrate as she opened the door, but then broke off abruptly. No islander had come seeking her. The British officer stood in the doorway, sharply outlined against the bright, moonlit sky. He was very tall, well over six foot, and built like an athlete, broad-shouldered and slim-waisted. Beneath his beret, Tansy could see dark hair, cut short, which set off a tanned face with clean-cut features, a strong chin and a firm mouth that could probably form a pleasant smile. The smile, however, was not in evidence at the moment. The dark eyes inspected her with a gaze so cool and enquiring that Tansy instinctively drew her head back into the shadows, only her body in the damply clinging sarong revealed in the lamplight.

'I'm looking for Dr Harland. Is he at home? Will you tell him Major Blake Aston would like to see him?' His voice was as firm as his appearance; it was also hard and unsympathetic.

Disconcerted at his unexpected visit, Tansy didn't answer straight away, and he said exasperatedly, 'Doesn't anyone on this damn island speak English?'

So the natives' trick had got under his skin already. Good! Then Tansy realised that in the sarong and with her hair hidden he mistook her, too, for one of the native girls. Impishly she tried to goad him further and said in execrable English, 'Medicine man, him not here.'

'So he took the trouble to teach at least one of you some English, did he? Where is he? When do you expect him back?'

Greatly enjoying herself, Tansy pretended not to understand at first and made him repeat the questions two or three times before answering, 'Him go 'way mighty canoe. He no come back many sunsets.'

The Major moved a little to one side to look at her more closely. 'Who are you?' he asked sharply. 'You're not the servant girl I saw this morning. Are you his woman?'

For a moment the bluntness of the question bereft Tansy of speech, and then, completely forgetting her role, she said tartly, 'I suppose *you* might call me that!'

Deliberately he let his eyes wander slowly down the curves of the sarong. 'The doctor has good taste,' he said softly.

Tansy felt herself blushing hotly. Really, the man was

despicable! Angrily she retorted, 'I must remember to tell him that when he returns. I'm sure he will be gratified by the approbation of such an *obvious* connoisseur!' Her stress of the word obvious turning it into a deliberate insult.

'Big words for a little native girl.' With a movement so quick that Tansy hardly realised he had made it, the Major reached across the threshold and pulled her out on to the veranda, while with the other hand he plucked the towel from her head. Tansy's hair fell upon her shoulders like liquid silver in the moonlight, framing her delicately featured face and clear, hazel eyes that were filled now with dismay as she realised that he had tricked her into giving herself away.

'Ah, I thought so. You're the girl I saw on the beach today. Who are you?' he demanded again.

'How dare you touch me! Please go away at once,' Tansy said angrily, ineffectively trying to shake off the hand that still held her arm in a casual grip that felt like a vice.

'Not until you tell me who you are—and where Dr Harland is,' he added as an afterthought. 'He knew we were coming here and was asked to give us every assistance in our work.'

'Ordered to, you mean!' Tansy exclaimed, losing her temper. 'Well, amazing as it may seem to you, Major Blake Aston, not everyone is willing to act like a tame sheep and sit idly by while you decide whether or not to tear this island apart so that you can play your war games. My father has gone to Australia to get you and your men removed from here. We don't want you on Aparoa, Major. Nobody wants you!'

The officer looked at her calmly, her angry words seeming to have had no effect on him at all, and Tansy bit her lip as she realised that she had blurted out more than she intended during her outburst.

'So he's your father, is he? Well, as he isn't here I shall have to make do with you instead. I need someone to act as an interpreter while we're surveying the island.'

Tansy stared at him. 'If you think I'll help you in what you're doing, you must be crazy!'

'Suit yourself, Miss Harland, but the people here might start getting worried when we begin our work.'

'What do you mean?' Tansy asked suspiciously. 'Why should they?'

With a slight sigh, as if he were lecturing a raw recruit, the Major said patiently, 'I shall be driving over and measuring up various stretches of land. The natives will be wondering what's happening and will start getting worried and anxious. If I had an interpreter to explain that this is simply an initial survey and that adequate compensation will be paid to anyone losing their land if we do decide to go ahead with an airstrip on Aparoa, then a great deal of unnecessary worry and distress would be avoided. Also, I would be able to answer any questions the people might want to ask me on the project. But of course, if you don't care about the natives, Miss Harland, then that's entirely up to you.'

'How dare you try to play on my feelings, use moral blackmail, to try to get me to help you?' Tansy said vehemently, appalled that this man could so calmly expect her to do just what he wanted at the lift of a finger. 'For your information, the natives already know why you're here, and you'll get as little co-operation from them as you will from me. Do your own dirty work, Major Aston!' Wrenching her arm away from him, Tansy stepped back into the house and went to slam the door in his face, but again he moved too quickly for her and put his foot in the doorway before she could shut it.

'Just a minute, I'm not finished with you yet,' he said grimly.

'Well, I have! I've said everything I ever intend to say to you. And don't ask me to help you again, because I won't, under any circumstances.'

'Very well, Miss Harland, if that's the way you want it. You're just going to make life tougher for everyone concerned,' he said harshly, for the first time showing anger at her defiant attitude. 'I shall ride as roughshod over this island and its people as I have to, and don't blame me if some get hurt in the process. A lot of hardship could be avoided and I could make this operation as painless as possible, but your stubborn attitude and the way you have obviously stirred up the natives to feel the same is going to make trouble unavoidable. And now that's all I have to say. Sleep on it, will you, Miss Harland? I'll call again in the morning.'

'Don't bother. My answer will still be the same.' And this time she did manage to slam the door, but there was little satisfaction in the action; she knew he could have prevented her if he had chosen to.

Tansy picked up the towel from where it had fallen and automatically continued to dry her hair. Drat the man! Why did he have to come here? And to ask her to help him of all things. That was the last thing she would ever do! Abstractedly she started to walk up and down the room. But he had sounded absolutely ruthless and he had proved that he could act ruthlessly too, in the way that he had handled the situation at the prison. By now the news of it would have spread throughout the entire island. Had he deliberately used his pistol to frighten the islanders into letting him do what he wanted, not only then but in the future?

Putting on a sweater and jeans and pushing her feet into a pair of sandals, Tansy let herself out of the back door into the warm night. After walking through the garden, she began to climb the hill behind the house, the way picked out easily in the silvered moonlight. At the top of the hill the ground levelled out into the huge, flat plateau that stretched from the cliff edge away into the dim interior of the island. It was here that the serried ranks of coconut palms that provided the main source of income for the natives had been planted under her father's guidance. Before he came to Aparoa the natives had each had their own small grove of trees, but now they had formed a co-operative and all shared the work and the profit made from the sale of copra.

The ground under the trees had been cleared so that the fallen nuts could be easily seen, and cattle allowed to graze on the grass to keep it short. Tansy saw several cows lying beneath the palms as she made her way to her favourite spot; a knoll of slightly higher ground on the edge of the cliffs where the flaming blossoms of flamboyant trees and the heady scents of bougainvillaeas made a perfect place to sit against a tree trunk and think in uninterrupted peace and to take in the beauty of the island and ocean. And tonight she needed to calm her nerves; that Aston man had set the seeds of doubt in her mind no matter how hard she tried to dismiss them. Would it be better for the islanders if she went along as an interpreter? The people were terribly possessive over their pieces of land, many of which had been handed down through countless generations. If they saw the soldiers taking measurements they would immediately jump to the conclusion that it was their land that was going to be put under layers of concrete. They would go running to Ruari, Tupuhoe, or herself and rumours would spread like wildfire. They would probably imagine the whole island under concrete before a day was out, Tansy thought ruefully, having no illusions about her fellow Aparoans.

Then there was the subject of compensation that the Major had mentioned. It was hard enough to get the natives to do any real work as it was, they were by nature extremely indolent, and if they thought that they would be paid for their land by the government they would immediately stop working altogether. They would insist that even the meanest patch of scrubland was worth a fortune and would spend all their time haggling over the price. And when they did get the money they would only fritter it away, Tansy reflected gloomily, remembering how they had once enthusiastically spent all their year's copra earnings on sets of golf clubs for the men and high-heeled shoes for the women that one enterprising trader had brought by schooner to the island in the hope of making a sale. Dr Harland had been furious, especially when women started breaking their ankles in the unsuitable shoes and the men began hitting each other with the golf clubs, finding them very efficient weapons.

Tansy sighed, wishing that her father were with her to ask his advice. She thought she heard the sound of a movement further down the hill and looked sharply in that direction. At first she could see nothing, but then, about twenty yards away, a cow climbed slowly to its feet and ambled off among the trees. Relaxing, Tansy settled back against the trunk of the tree again and looked out across the bay. The view of the ocean was framed in palm trees, their fronds whispering gently in the warm winds of the gulf stream, under a moon so brilliant that the night seemed day.

Slowly Tansy straightened up. It was against all her

inclinations, but she knew that when Major Aston came the next day she would have to act as his interpreter, however much she would hate doing it. Then a reassuring thought came to her; perhaps by going with him she might be able to discourage the soldiers, point out how unsuitable the place was for their purposes. And she would certainly be able to calm the natives' fears and urge them to be as unhelpful as possible, she thought more cheerfully. Yes, Major Aston certainly wasn't going to have things all his own way after all!

She turned and began to make her way down the familiar path towards home, but as she went she had the eerie feeling that she was being watched and turned several times to look behind her. But there was nothing there, only the swaying palms and the sleeping cattle. She gave herself a little shake and mentally berated herself for being silly. The arrival of the soldiers had already begun to play on her nerves.

# CHAPTER TWO

THE next morning Tansy woke very early as usual, but already Inara was ahead of her. Tansy could hear the native woman in the kitchen as she sang while she prepared breakfast. As a rule the women were more energetic than the men, but they still did as little housework as possible, preferring to spend their time gossiping or making innumerable dresses and sarongs on the sewing machines that were proud possessions in every household, but Inara had been devoted to David Harland ever since he had saved her mother's life several years ago, and now she came happily every day to cook and look after his house for him.

Pushing open the window, Tansy looked across to the twenty-foot-high walls of the prison. Already there were signs of activity there, smoke from cooking fires drifted up to where a few white clouds hung motionless in a sky whose indigo was lighting to azure as the sun rose higher. So Major Aston knew that in a tropical climate the best hours in which to work were those early in the morning. Hurrying downstairs, Tansy told Inara that she would be going with the soldiers and to spread the word that she would hold a clinic later in the day. She knew that the islanders would have no trouble in reaching her in an emergency—they would be so curious about the soldiers' activities that there would probably be a crowd of them trailing the jeep wherever it went.

As she did every morning, Tansy walked down through the garden that her father had so lovingly

21

planted and which bloomed abundantly in this ideal climate. Single and double hibiscus grew alongside roses of every hue, giant-headed blue and pink hydrangeas blossomed beside a myriad gorgeous azaleas, and surrounding them all were frangipani trees, brilliant flamboyants and the inevitable spreading purple bougainvillaeas. Rounding a bend in the path, she came to a break in the side of the hill where a small waterfall, about fifteen feet high, fell into a shallow rock pool with flowers growing all around the banks and in the crevices of the rocks. The fall made a natural shower and, after pinning up her hair, Tansy took off her sarong and stepped under it, enjoying the invigorating feeling of the cold water that flowed down from the mountain.

As she washed she whistled to herself as she did each morning; having been brought up by her father after the death of the mother she tried in vain to remember, Tansy had developed quite a few boyish traits that her years of medical training in London had entirely failed to eradicate. Stepping from the pool, she reached up to where she had hung the sarong on a convenient branch, and then hastily held it in front of her, a look of startled horror on her face as she heard a noise and saw Blake Aston coming round a bend in the path. He came to a stop, an amused lift to his mouth as he noted her discomfiture. Tansy expected him to apologise for intruding on her privacy and to go quickly away again, but the insufferable man merely leaned his long length up against a tree trunk, folded his arms, and stood there, casually watching her.

For a minute Tansy stared at him speechlessly, then she said through clenched teeth, 'Will you please go away?'

'Oh, I don't mind waiting,' he said affably, but with a mocking gleam in his dark eyes.

'Can't you see that I want to get dressed?' If the man

was trying to goad her into losing her temper he was certainly succeeding.

'Oh, don't mind me, Miss Harland. When you've seen one, you've seen them all!' he said outrageously.

'Oh!' Tansy gasped. 'Why, you—you ...' She was unable to find words to express her feelings.

The Major grinned. 'Do I take it that you're trying to tell me that I'm not behaving like an officer and a gentleman?'

'That's exactly what I mean,' she said vehemently.

'But, Miss Harland, I thought you liked to play games. Why else did you pretend that you were a native girl last night?'

'Because I didn't want to talk to you,' Tansy retorted. 'Because I ...' she broke off, then went on slowly, 'Oh, I see. You intend to go on standing there until I apologise for last night, is that it?'

'That's the general idea,' he agreed.

'How did you know I came here to bathe?'

'I heard a woman whistling. It was so very unladylike that I was sure it must be you, so I followed my ears. It was pure chance.' He paused. 'But if it hadn't been this way it would have been some other.'

He had spoken softly, but there had been a distinct menace in his voice, and Tansy realised that he would be a far more dangerous person to cross than she had so confidently supposed at first. She shivered slightly despite the heat and said coldly, 'Really, Major, this has gone far enough. You're becoming ridiculous.'

Implacably he answered, 'I've got plenty of time, Miss Harland, and I'm not going to turn my back until I have your apology for your rudeness last night.' And he settled his broad shoulders more comfortably against the tree.

Tansy glared at him defiantly. How dared he treat her

as if she were in the wrong! 'Then you can just go to hell!' she said furiously, and presenting as little of herself to him as she decently could, she hastily draped the sarong round her and tucked it in, at the same time shaking her head so that her hair fell free of the restraining pins. Then she turned to face him, confident that she had kept herself hidden from his sight. 'I rather think you lost that round, Major,' she said triumphantly.

'Did I?' There was an appreciative gleam in his eyes and a humorous lift to his mouth that Tansy didn't like. He couldn't have seen, could he? she wondered as she looked at him. The Major saw the sudden doubt in her eyes and his grin became even broader, but he didn't pursue the point. He indicated the sarong. 'Don't you have any European clothes to wear, or have you gone completely native?'

'What I wear is nothing to do with you!'

'It is when you're going to be among my men for any length of time. They've been away from home a long time, Miss Harland, and I don't want them getting any ideas when they see you running around with only that scrap of material covering you.'

'Lots of island women wear sarongs,' Tansy protested.

'But the rest of the island women haven't got your face, your hair and your figure,' he replied bluntly.

Tansy glared up at him, but he looked back at her steadily until she felt her colour heightening. Turning away, she began to walk back through the garden towards the house and he fell into step behind her. When she thought about it, Tansy supposed that in a way he was right; she had been used to wearing a sarong since she was a little child, and it came completely naturally to her, but, as she was an English girl, the soldiers would expect her to behave differently from the other island woman. She sniffed exasperatedly; not only was Blake Aston telling her what to do, he was also telling her what to wear, and the worst part of it was that the horrible man was right!

Arriving at the veranda, she turned to face him. 'Anyway, what makes you think that I'm going to come with you to speak to the islanders?'

He rested his hand on the rail. 'You may be incredibly naïve, but you're not insensitive. You'll come. I'll wait outside for you in the jeep. And be as quick as you can, will you? I've already wasted enough time and I want to get as much done as possible before the heat becomes oppressive.' And he swung away to walk out to the road, leaving Tansy to stare after him furiously.

So he had wasted enough time, had he? although back at the pool he had seemed in no particular hurry. Tansy wondered just what he would have done if she had continued to hold out against him, then decided that perhaps it would be better not to think about that. With a man as unpredictable as Major Aston anything might have happened. Going to her room, she changed into a short-sleeved shirt and a pair of slacks; banging drawers and noisily shutting cupboard doors as she thought of the Major. He was the most overbearing, conceited, self-assured, arrogant man she had ever met! Never in all her life had she felt such instant antagonism towards anyone. Anger surged up in her until she had to sit down and clench her fists in an effort to control herself. This wouldn't do; she mustn't let her emotions take over. Deliberately she took up her hairbrush and brushed her hair until it shone like quicksilver, the soothing motion settling her nerves. She must keep all her wits about her if she wanted to outsmart Major Aston and get him and his men off Aparoa as quickly as possible. And right now she could think of nothing she wanted more!

There were three men waiting in the jeep outside the house. The driver was a private, but sitting next to him in the front was a lieutenant, whom Blake Aston introduced as John Andrews, a young man a year or two younger than Tansy's own age of twenty-five, with brown hair and an eager expression on his open face. He gallantly helped her to get into the back seat next to the Major, but Tansy took care to sit as far away from him as possible. There was an amused quirk on his lips as he ran his eyes over her clothes and noticed her rebellious attitude, but he said nothing. The men had been studying a large-scale map of the island and now Blake ordered the driver to go along the coastal road that almost circled the island with one or two dips inland to ford the rivers.

They set off along the red, dusty road and almost immediately were followed by a throng of children which grew bigger as they approached the village. This was the largest village on the island, built near the easy passage to the open sea so that the men could go fishing. The buildings were grouped round a large, open, grassy space, and comprised a hundred or so huts thatched with grass, reeds or leaves on solid wooden frameworks, but occasionally there were bungalows or houses made of stone, wood, and galvanised iron. The few stone houses had mainly been built by convict labour to house the prison warders and were grouped nearer to the prison, while Ruari and Tupuhoe lived in a wooden, European style house in the centre of the village. On slightly higher ground on the eastern side there was a stone-built church where the islanders gathered on Sundays to sing hymns and exchange the latest gossip. The minister came only once every six months or so to perform baptisms and to marry any of the islanders who had lived together long

enough and had had enough children to decide that there
was now little risk of them getting tired of one another.
Near Tupuhoe's house there was also a village assembly
house where everyone met to discuss any momentous
decisions, and which also doubled as a trading post and
as a school, which Ruari was slowly persuading the
children to attend.

Tansy had never driven round the island in a motor-
ised vehicle before and it seemed strange to see all the
familiar landmarks going past so quickly. Usually David
Harland drove himself round in a small pony trap with
just enough room for Tansy to squeeze in beside him,
but Tansy mostly used an old upright bicycle to get
from one village to another. Soon they drove down a
steep road to another village where the driver blew his
horn energetically to clear the way.

'Oh, you shouldn't have done that,' Tansy said in-
voluntarily.

Blake Aston looked at her. 'Why not?'

'Because now every time the jeep stops all the children
will want to do it.'

The Major laughed, a full masculine laugh, that
would have been extremely attractive in anyone else.
Tansy just wished it *had* been someone else—she would
rather have been anywhere than have to sit next to this
particular man for hours on end. They stopped in the
village and Blake and the Lieutenant got out of the jeep
to go and look at the shoreline while Tansy was amused
to watch the villagers, torn between following the soldiers
or coming to Tansy to find out what it was all about.
Patiently she answered their eager questions. Yes, the
soldiers were going to look all round the island. No, they
didn't need a guide—they had a map. Tansy explained
what a map was, showed it to them and listened to them

laugh delightedly as she pointed out their own village. Was that really them on that small dot?

The driver, meanwhile, was having a hectic time trying to stop the children from climbing in the jeep and touching everything that moved. Eventually, of course, one child's eager fingers found the horn and they continued to sound it until the officers returned. Tansy sat blandly in the back; she could have stopped the children with a word, but why should she spoil their fun, especially if it annoyed the Major? But it didn't seem to annoy him at all, he simply smiled at the children and lifted them gently from the vehicle. Tansy watched him without lessening her dislike of him one iota; he was probably only doing it to impress the villagers anyway, she thought sardonically.

'Do the islanders do much fishing in the lagoon itself?' he asked her as they started off again.

'Yes, they net lobsters and take the canoes out to spear the big fish, or else they take a pail to catch inaa; they're tiny fish, only about half an inch long, and you eat them whole, cooked in a paste of flour and water and fried. They taste a bit like your herrings,' she told him.

He raised an eyebrow slightly at the 'your'. 'I gather you consider yourself to be an Aparoan, Miss Harland?'

'Yes, of course. I've lived here most of my life.'

He nodded and seemed to file the information away before going on to ask other things about the island. Tansy found herself pointing out the small bush clearings around the villages where taro, yams and cassava were grown. 'The taro can only be grown in those marshy pits, but yams are easier and grow to enormous sizes,' she informed him, her eyes bright as she talked eagerly of her beloved island. 'They can be stored for months too, so they're regarded as a form of wealth—

like having money in the bank. Then cassava—that's tapioca—grows on hilly soils, while sago, breadfruit and bananas grow near the jungle.'

Tansy stopped for breath, expecting to see a look of derision in the Major's eyes at her enthusiasm, but he was watching her seriously, looking as if he was really interested in everything she was telling him. He told the driver to pull up on the top of a cliff where they had a good view of the southern half of the island and, helping Tansy out of the jeep, led her away from the others nearer to the cliff edge.

'That passageway through the coral reef opposite the main village—it's shown on the map as the only way to get to the island. Is that correct?' he asked, unfolding the map.

'Yes, although there are one or two smaller ones on the windward side, big enough for a canoe but not for a boat of any size. The schooners never go there. And the lagoon near the old jetty isn't very deep now, either. There was an earthquake about thirty years ago, part of the cliffs fell into the sea and the harbour has been silting up ever since. I don't suppose even the schooners will be able to tie up there soon. They will have to anchor out in the lagoon and do all the unloading by dinghy,' she added dampeningly.

Blake went to sit down under a nearby palm tree to study the map and Tansy went to stand near him uncertainly. He looked up. 'For heaven's sake sit down, woman. I don't bite,' he said irritably.

Tight-lipped, Tansy did so, wishing fervently that she had been a man with shoulders as broad as Ruari's. Not that even Ruari's muscles could have been guaranteed to overcome the ogre beside her, she admitted reluctantly.

'You paint a very black picture for our hopes of

making a deep-water harbour, Miss Harland,' Blake Aston mused, stroking his chin as he perused the map.

'Oh, I'm quite certain it wouldn't be any good at all,' Tansy hastened to assure him. 'The depths given on your map are hopelessly out of date. They must have been taken from some very old charts drawn up when the jetty was first built. I'm sure that no new soundings have been taken since the earthquake.'

'And there's no other piece of coastline that would be at all suitable?'

'No, none,' Tansy replied emphatically, leaning towards him in her eagerness to convince him.

Blake turned his head and for a moment dark eyes looked deep into hazel. Tansy felt suddenly, unaccountably, breathless.

Folding up the map, Blake got easily to his feet. 'Then it's a good job that we have dredging machines and explosives at our disposal. Clearing the harbour again and widening the passage through the coral should present no problem at all.'

Tansy stared up to where he towered above her, making no move to take the hand that he held out to help her up. Incredulously she said, 'Then those questions you asked me about the depth of the lagoon; you didn't really want to know?'

'No, they were quite irrelevant. I just wanted to see how far you would go to keep us off Aparoa. From now on I shall know that I can't trust any piece of information you give me.'

'But it's true!' Tansy protested, getting to her feet to face him. 'The harbour is much shallower than it was.'

'So shallow that schooners will have to stop tying up there?' he asked derisively. 'How strange, when a schooner captain I spoke to only last week told me that there was a good twenty feet under his keel when he took a sounding on his last visit!'

Tansy stared at him in consternation. He had set a trap for her and she had walked neatly into it. Then she remembered that he had said he would use explosives to deepen the lagoon, and she caught at his sleeve as he went to turn away.

'Wait, please,' she said earnestly, and he turned back, an impatient frown on his forehead. 'You can't use explosives in the harbour. That's where the natives dive for mother-of-pearl mussels and trochus shells. It's one of the few means we have, other than copra, of raising money for imported goods. We sell the mother-of-pearl and the shells to Japan for button-making. If you use explosives it will ruin the mussel beds completely.' She raised long-lashed eyes to him pleadingly, but the Major merely looked down at her with an expression of open disbelief on his face.

'It's true, I tell you!' Tansy clenched her fists impatiently as she tried to make him understand how much this mattered. 'You can ask anyone—they'll all tell you the same.'

'But I can't ask anyone else, can I? No one else speaks English, except you.'

'I'll translate for you. I'll take you to ...' Then she broke off her eager assurances as she saw the expression on his face and realised that he no longer trusted her, because she'd exaggerated about the harbour.

'Exactly,' he said softly.

Without a word, Tansy turned and walked back towards the jeep, repeatedly blaming herself for having so stupidly walked into the trap he had set so neatly for her. Now he would never believe anything she said, no matter how true or how important to the islanders. Abstractedly she got into the jeep and Lieutenant Andrews came over to talk to her.

He had addressed at least three remarks to her before Tansy roused herself enough to pay him any attention and she realised that he was asking her about the many shells to be found on Aparoa.

'Oh, oh yes. There are some beautiful ones. I believe that one or two really rare ones have been found occasionally,' she said with only half her mind on the conversation.

'Where would be the best place to find them?'

'Oh—on the fringe reefs after the tide has gone out, I should think.'

'Fringe reefs?' he asked in puzzlement. 'You mean the big-coral reefs all round the island?'

'No, those are barrier reefs.' It was obvious that the Lieutenant hadn't been to a Pacific island before. Patiently Tansy explained that the fringe reefs grew on the shelving shoreline and were made smooth by constant wave action so that it was possible to walk on them. 'You'll see the native women out on them every day collecting shellfish from the pools and crevices,' Tansy told him. 'That's where my father always goes when he looks for shells. There, and among the rocks at the base of the cliffs.'

'That's marvellous. I'll go along there as soon as Blake gives me a bit of time off.'

Tansy looked at him thoughtfully, suddenly realising that she might possibly be able to influence the Major through his Lieutenant. She gave John Andrews a smile that had dazzled more than one man back in England. 'My father has quite a large variety of shells that he has collected over the years. Perhaps you would like to see them?'

'Would I! I say, that's awfully kind of you. When may I come?' he asked eagerly.

Tansy laughed. 'I'm busy this afternoon, but you can come to dinner this evening if you like. I'll ask our cook to prepare some native food for you. That's if the Major will let you off the hook, of course.'

'The Major will consider it,' said a dry voice behind them, and John Andrews immediately snapped to attention as Blake rejoined them.

They visited two more villages that day and Tansy did her best to allay the villagers' fears while Blake and John went off to survey the terrain, but towards noon he called a halt for the day and drove Tansy back to her home.

'Thank you for your services, Miss Harland,' he said formally, and then surprised her by adding, 'I'll call for you again tomorrow morning, if I may.'

For a moment Tansy hestitated, wondering why he bothered to ask her if he wasn't going to believe anything she said. Then she realised that from his point of view nothing had changed; he still needed an interpreter.

'Very well, Major. I'll see you tomorrow.'

'Er—Major, you were going to consider ...' John broke in hopefully.

'Ah, yes. Very well, Lieutenant, if Miss Harland is willing to put up with you, you may as well go,' he consented.

The prig! Tansy thought, like a teacher letting a small boy have a treat. Maliciously she smiled at John and said, 'I shall look forward to that, *John*,' emphasising his christian name. 'It will be fun to be with someone my own age.'

But if the dig had gone home Blake Aston didn't

show it, merely raising a hand in salute before telling the driver to carry on.

Hastily Tansy stepped back from the cloud of dust thrown up by the jeep's wheels and went into the house to collect her sarong and go and shower under the garden waterfall again. Although she despised him, she somehow couldn't shake Blake Aston out of her mind. Was he really so insensitive to the needs of the islanders that he would deliberately destroy one of their main sources of livelihood? Somehow Tansy thought that he was not only insensitive, but could be completely ruthless if he found it necessary to achieve his own ends. From the way he had led her on to exaggerate about the silting in the harbour, it was obvious that he was a student of human nature and it wouldn't be long before he began to suspect that the natives weren't as against him as Tansy had led him to believe. They loved to see all the wonders of the more sophisticated world and would spend days on end watching other people work, especially if it required no effort from themselves. Already the few islanders that Tansy had spoken to had been not unfriendly in their attitude towards the soldiers and would have made them welcome if she hadn't intervened. They would be in for a very rude awakening if Blake did decide that Aparoa was suitable for use as a base.

But somehow she must prevent him from finding the island suitable. She cheered up slightly when she recalled that the NATO forces also needed an airstrip. Well, there certainly wasn't anywhere on the island that could remotely be used as a runway, as the Major would find out tomorrow. In the meantime, she would do her best to use John Andrews as her mouthpiece in convincing Blake to submit an unfavourable report. But she must be subtle in her approach, she realised, it wouldn't do for nice Lieutenant Andrews to know he was being used, however worthy the cause.

Back in the house she found Inara waiting with her lunch and with a barrage of questions about the soldiers. Tansy was used to this and told her as much as she could, while omitting any mention of blasting the harbour; that she would tell to Ruari but to no one else at the moment. With luck their fears might yet come to nothing and there was no sense in unduly alarming everyone unnecessarily. Before going down to the clinic, Tansy asked Inara to prepare a special meal for the evening, telling her that the young officer was coming to dinner, then smiled at the native woman's reaction. She knew that before an hour was up the news would be all over the village.

She smiled again as she remembered her dig at the Major, when she had stressed the difference in their ages. But there probably wasn't that much difference, she mused as she walked down to the clinic, which was almost hidden among a group of graceful pandanus palms. She guessed that Blake Aston was about thirty-five, but his long experience of being in charge of men, his self-assurance and air of decisiveness combined to make him appear older, especially in comparison with John.

The clinic was a busy one with lots more questions to answer until Tansy felt as if her throat was drying up, and it was something of a relief to get out the pony and trap to go slowly over part of the road she had already covered so speedily that morning to visit some patients in outlying villages who were too ill to be brought to the clinic. By the time she got back and had unharnessed and fed the pony, there was only time to change into a sleeveless blue cotton dress before John was knocking at the door.

'Hallo. Do come in,' Tansy smiled as she opened the door.

Obviously he hadn't known quite what to expect of a house on a tropical island and appeared somewhat reassured when he saw the beautifully polished antique furniture that her father had brought with him to Aparoa. 'Why, you've got electric light, Miss Harland!' he exclaimed.

'Yes, we have our own generator. But please call me Tansy. Would you like a drink?'

She poured herself a dry Martini but handed John a toddy, a liquor obtained by fermenting the sap from the flower buds of the coconut palms. He took a good swallow and Tansy had a hard job to keep from laughing at the expression that suddenly appeared on his face as the taste hit him. Manfully he tried not to let his feelings show and said, in a somewhat strangled voice, 'Very nice. Er—what is it, exactly?'

Then Tansy laughed openly. 'It's all right, it grows on you. Another couple of swallows and you'll really start to enjoy it. Come on, I'll show you Daddy's shells before we have dinner.'

She led the way into her father's 'den', a room completely cluttered with a miscellaneous assortment of items that her father had found of interest, from the jawbones of a shark to a shelf full of rootoos, grotesque native masks of jungle gods carved from coconut logs which the islanders once used to decorate the corners of their houses. Going to a cabinet-like piece of furniture, Tansy pulled open one or two of the shallow drawers and showed John the shells that shone against the dark velvet lining. The colours and intricacies of shape were breathtaking, a rainbow profusion in fragile heaps of pink, blue and mauve; round, long, with jagged spikes, striped, spotted or plain, the shells lay in glittering confusion.

'I'm afraid my father never really got round to collating them,' Tansy apologised as she pulled out more drawers for him to see. 'He just liked them for what they were. But if you're really interested he has several books on the subject which you would be welcome to borrow.'

But John was already happily picking up shells to hold them to the light. 'But these are exquisite,' he said enthusiastically. 'Oh, I know this one. It's a conch, isn't it?' he asked, taking one of the largest shells from a deep bottom drawer.

'Yes, that one has a history attached to it. The natives use the giant conch shells as horns and sound them as a warning. That one is supposed to have been blown when the convicts mutinied over a hundred years ago.'

Tansy went on to describe the other shells as best she could, for she was no expert, and it seemed no time at all before Inara came to tell them that dinner was ready. Inara had always been an excellent cook, but tonight she had surpassed herself. There was soup, followed by grilled freshwater shrimps caught far up the island's rivers, and a lobster on a bed of rice with an endive salad. For dessert they had tender shoots of coconut palm sliced wafer-thin.

During the meal, Tansy kept John's glass topped up with toddy, which, as she had prophesied, his palate had got used to and he was obviously enjoying. When she could steer the conversation away from shells, she tried to impress on him in a roundabout way how happy the islanders were and would continue to be if only they were left in peace, how the establishment of a base would completely wreck their present way of life. She daren't push her point too hard, but John seemed a nice enough person, with some thought to the feelings of others, and she was satisfied when she said goodnight to him later that some of her persuasiveness had made itself felt.

'It's been a marvellous evening. Thank you so much. May I come again?' he asked ingenuously.

Tansy smiled. 'Yes, of course. Come whenever you have some free time. But I'll see you in the morning, won't I?'

'No, I'm afraid not. Blake is sending me to the lagoon to take soundings from the boat. He wants me to see if it will be possible to use another part for a harbour, away from the mussel beds.'

'Oh!' Tansy was taken aback. 'When did he tell you to do that?'

'This afternoon. He spent several hours poring over the maps and charts, then gave me this assignment for tomorrow morning.'

This piece of news had really given Tansy something to think about as she climbed the hill to her favourite spot looking out over the sea. It was the last thing she would have expected the Major to do—to waste time on looking for an alternative site just to try to save the natives' source of income, small though it was in comparison to the huge amounts of money that would be needed to move the harbour further along the coastline. Somehow it hardly seemed in character for Blake Aston. And yet— Tansy tried hard to be fair—how much did she really know about his true character? She had been biased against him from the start, had given him little or no chance to behave other than in the overbearing manner he had assumed towards her, although his attitude to the islanders had always been courteous after the bad start when he first arrived. Tansy sighed; could she have misjudged him?

When she walked back down the hill eventually, she had made up her mind to give the Major the benefit of the doubt; she would try to treat him less like a hated intruder and endeavour to see things from his point of view, or at least with an open mind.

# CHAPTER THREE

This praiseworthy attempt at fairmindedness was, however, rudely shattered less than twenty-four hours later. The Major had collected her the next morning, accompanied by the driver and a corporal this time, and they had driven, often over roads that were no more than dirt tracks, round the interior of the island. Tansy had tried to be fair—how she'd tried! She had greeted him with a smile and answered all his questions as fully as she could, often giving pieces of information that she thought would be useful to him. His glances at her had been sceptical at first, but gradually his manner had eased and she found him very observant and possessed of a dry sense of humour. Once or twice she even found herself laughing at a witty comment or an anecdote about the army. The morning was, in fact, going along well. Tansy was beginning to realise how much she missed the company of people like Blake Aston, people whose companionship she had enjoyed during her years in London, but the memory of which had gradually faded after her return to Aparoa.

That was until they reached the coconut plantation on the long plateau that stretched inland from the cliffs. Blake got out of the jeep and ordered the men to take their equipment and start measuring up the area.

'Who does the plantation belong to?' he asked her.

'To the whole island. When my father came here he persuaded everyone to form a co-operative and they began to plant these trees. It's really only starting to pay

40

off now because it takes eight to ten years before the palms get big enough to grow nuts, but then they keep producing them for about seventy years.' Tansy glanced up to the trees that towered over fifty feet in the air, looking rather like rows of ballet dancers with fantastic headdresses. In the distance some natives were collecting the fallen nuts or gathering ripe ones from the trees, not by climbing up them and throwing down the nuts as their ancestors had done, but with the help of a very long pole with an iron hook on the end. Now the only time anyone tried to climb the palms was on festive occasions when the young men showed off their skill and strength before the village maidens.

'What's the process for turning the nuts into copra?' Blake enquired.

'When the nuts are gathered, the men split them open and remove the flesh and then leave it to dry in the sun for several days; that's when it becomes copra. Then it's bagged and stored in sheds to await the next schooner,' Tansy told him as he leaned negligently against the side of the jeep. 'But that isn't the only part that's utilised; the leaves are used for thatching houses and weaving mats and baskets, and the fibres we use for rope and for fuel for cooking fires—oh, its uses are endless. The islanders are hoping to have enough money this year to build a proper drying shed where the copra can be spread on racks over a closed-in fire. Then it dries out in only a day and you get a much better quality of copra.'

Then Tansy stopped, aware that her enthusiastic tongue had run away with her again. 'I'm sorry. You must find this very uninteresting,' she apologised.

'On the contrary. You know your subject well, and to hear an expert speak is always interesting.'

Tansy flushed at the compliment. 'Oh, I'm no expert.

You should hear Daddy when he gets going.'

'I should like to—but he's still in Australia trying to get rid of us, isn't he?' he said with a wry twist to his mouth.

A quick retort came to Tansy's lips, but she bit it back, remembering her resolve to try to be fair. And after all, what he had said was in fact true.

'The natives have a legend of how the coconut came into being,' she hastily reverted to their former topic. 'They say that once there was nothing but bushes and grass on the island and a woman called Hina, and her husband, Tuna, were very sad about this. So the man said, "When I die cut off my head and plant it." So when Tuna died she did as he asked, and soon a green shoot appeared which grew into a huge tree with nuts the same shape as Tuna's head. When Hina picked a nut and took off the fibre, she found three marks exactly where Tuna's eyes and mouth would have been, and, if you look, you'll find that every coconut has those same marks.'

Blake smiled, a rather whimsical smile, as Tansy looked up at him. 'That's a nice story. A bedtime story.'

'You'll have to tell it to your children when you go back home,' Tansy said lightly.

'I'm afraid I shall have to save it for quite some time, then. I'm not married, Miss Harland.'

'Oh.' For some irrational reason Tansy wasn't displeased at this piece of information. 'I thought you would be at your . . .' She stopped herself quickly.

'At my age,' he finished for her drily. 'There may be an age gap between us, Miss Harland, as you took care to point out to me, but I'm not quite in my dotage yet.'

'No, I didn't think you were.' Tansy looked up into his eyes and found them watching her speculatively. 'Why aren't you married?' she asked abruptly.

He hesitated for a long moment and Tansy realised just how personal her question had been and thought he was going to ignore it. But then he said slowly, seriously, 'Because it would take a very special kind of woman to tolerate the kind of life I lead. She would need to marry my job as well as me—the constant moves and long separations, the possibility of more or less having to bring up children by herself and to cope with all the problems while I'm away. Not many women would be happy in that kind of role—unless the man meant more to them than anything else, that is. And I'm afraid that leaves seldom last long enough to meet someone and have time for a permanent relationship of that type to grow.'

As Tansy listened she wondered if she had misjudged him even more than she thought and whether he was ever lonely.

Perhaps compassion showed in her face, for there was a wicked gleam in Blake's eyes as his mood changed and he said, 'But in the meantime I do my best to go through the field to find a suitable candidate. Why don't you apply for the position?'

'Me? Don't be silly!' Tansy was disconcerted.

He gave her a sudden smile that was as attractive as she had imagined it might be. 'Why not? It would be interesting finding out if we were compatible,' he said outrageously, but looking her up and down, added, 'But then you are rather skinny—I do prefer a woman who has some flesh to get hold of.'

'I'm not skinny!' Tansy retorted indignantly, rising to the bait. 'I'm fashionably slender.'

'Is that what you call it?' Blake was unimpressed. 'Then there's this age difference you keep on about. How old are you, twenty-one, twenty-two?'

'No, I'm twenty-five. I just look younger than my age.'

'Hm, that's better, admittedly. But I expect you're completely inexperienced and I'd have to teach you all there is to know. But I'm willing to give it a try.'

He had taken a purposeful step towards her and to her horror had gone to put his hands on her shoulders to draw her towards him, when there was a hastily suppressed laugh behind them and she turned to see the corporal hovering nearby, a big grin splitting his face until Blake turned towards him.

'Take that silly grin off your face, Corporal, or I'll give you a reason to wipe it off!'

'Sir!' The corporal saluted, his face a frozen mask, and Tansy hurriedly got in the jeep, her cheeks flushed beneath her tan.

The men talked together for a few moments before Blake came to sit beside her again, and as she looked up at him uncertainly, she saw imps of merriment in his dark eyes. So he *had* been teasing her; just as she suspected. But all the same she couldn't help wondering just what might have happened if the corporal hadn't returned at that moment. Would he have kissed her? Or would she have called his bluff? Perhaps it was just as well that she would never find out; Tansy had been kissed by many boy-friends in England, but somehow she felt that their kisses would pale into insignificance beside Blake's undoubted experience. Still, she reluctantly admitted to herself, he was right; it would have been interesting to find out.

She had been so absorbed in her thoughts that she hardly realised that they were now nearing the place where another shorter plateau branched off at right angles from the plantation. This area had not yet been cleared and was half jungle, half scrub, an area of nature growing free and wild.

'How far does this plateau reach?' Blake asked her, reverting to his more formal manner.

'I'm not sure. About half a mile, I should think, but it's quite wide. You can't drive through it, though, the undergrowth is too dense and it doesn't lead anywhere.'

'Hm.' He studied the map and wrote in some figures Tansy didn't understand, although she craned over to see. 'Miss Harland, I'm going to ask the driver to take you home while the corporal and I survey this area on foot.'

'You won't need me any more today?' There was just the slightest hint of disappointment in Tansy's voice.

'No, but thank you for your help. It's been very useful.' As he looked at her Tansy saw warmth in his eyes for the first time.

She was not displeased, therefore, when, in the early evening, she heard a knock on the door and went to open it expecting to see John, but found Blake standing there instead.

'Oh, Major Aston! I thought it was John,' she said in surprise. 'Won't you come in?'

He paused for a second, but then stepped into the room, ducking his head slightly to avoid the low, beamed ceiling.

'Oh, dear,' Tansy said laughingly. 'I'm afraid these houses weren't designed for anyone as tall as you. Can I get you a drink, Major?'

'No, thank you.'

It came to Tansy then that there was something strange about his manner; incredibly he seemed ill at ease, as if he was making up his mind to say something, and she suddenly felt a chill down her spine.

'What is it? Why have you come here?' she demanded.

'I wanted to tell you myself, Miss Harland. After you left this morning we surveyed the coconut plantation area very thoroughly. It will make an ideal site for an airstrip. It has the added advantage that the plateau running at right angles to it towards the east could be used as a cross-strip so that we could have an all-wind landing area.'

Tansy was staring at him aghast, hardly able to believe what her senses told her. 'But the trees—the coconut palms?' she managed.

'They will all have to come down,' he answered bluntly.

She flinched at the brutality of his words and leant back against the table, her legs feeling suddenly weak.

'I should also tell you that Lieutenant Andrews made a thorough inspection of the lagoon today, but found nowhere else that could possibly be used as a harbour. The present one would have to be blasted and dredged.'

'So you've left us with nothing?' Tansy said dully.

Blake's mouth set in a firm line. 'I'm sorry.'

'Sorry! How dare you say you're sorry!' Anger kept the tears from her eyes. 'You walk in here and tell me that you're going to kill this island, and all you can say is you're sorry!'

'Two other islands are also being surveyed. When the reports are considered they may choose one of those instead,' he said stiffly.

'Oh, don't try to sop me off with that. You don't want a different island to be chosen. You want it to be Aparoa because it will be a feather in your cap to have found it. What will they do—promote you to Colonel?' Tansy was almost shouting now in her rage and frustration. 'And to think that I tried to be open-minded and fair towards you today! My God, I bet you were laughing up your sleeve at every bit of information I gave you. Playing me along, even indulging in a little light flirtation to soften me up, while all the time you were planning to push this island for all you were worth so that the brass hats could look on you as one of their bright boys!' she jibed cruelly.

There was a set look on Blake's face as he said grimly, 'I've told you this because I think you have a right to know. You can inform your father if you wish, but I'm afraid he won't be able to exert much influence in the decision. This is too important.'

'And the natives? Am I to tell them?' she asked angrily, her voice filled with bitterness. 'Or is this thing *too important* for the people whose lives it will ruin to know about?'

'I'd rather you didn't. You might only be alarming them unnecessarily. As I said, Aparao might not be chosen. And I would ask you to think about it carefully before you tell them.'

'Oh, I'll think about it. I could hardly think about anything else, could I?' Tansy's knuckles were white as she stood facing him, trembling with fury. 'But I tell you this, Blake Aston, if I do tell the natives, then you and your men will be lucky to leave this island alive! Now get out of my house. I don't ever want to see you again!'

It was quite some time after Blake had turned sharply on his heel and walked out of the house before Tansy roused herself from the armchair into which she had sunk as soon as he had gone. She felt strangely numb from the shock he had inflicted and her thoughts and emotions were a chaotic mixture of hurt pride and mental anguish. But from it all came one emotion that overrode everything else; it was hatred, pure and deep, for the man who had brought this on the island. The irrationality of the hate made it all the worse, because she couldn't combat it with reason. She had started to like

him, started to trust him. Heavens, she had even wondered what it would be like if he had in fact kissed her!
But now it was as if he had struck her repeatedly in the
face, leaving wounds that were raw and ragged and
would leave scars that would only fade and never heal.
As Tansy sat there with her head in her hands, she
realised for the first time that she was capable of intense
emotion. She changed in that hour from a girl to a
woman, but tragically what had changed her was not
love, but hate.

At length she got up and went into the garden, but
tonight the heavy scents were cloying and overpowered
her senses. Turning, she made her way down to the shore
to feel the cool sea breeze and took off her sandals to
walk in the soft white coral sand. The brilliant scarlet
and gold and copper of the setting sun were softened in
the sea's reflection, which shimmered dreamily as the
slow breakers slid in to shore. Dully she realised that
she had behaved like a complete fool as far as Blake
Aston was concerned; he was a professional soldier and,
as such, was interested in nothing else but furthering his
own career. He had said he would ride roughshod over
the islanders, and she was an islander, wasn't she? Someone whom he had made use of when he needed her. He
was callous, completely unsympathetic to the needs of
others, and entirely ruthless in his driving ambition. He
had to be; for anyone else would have realised that the
harbour and the plantation were the Aparoans' only
sources of livelihood and would have immediately sent
in a report saying that the island was wholly unsuitable.
The only discordant note in the whole affair was that
the Major had bothered to come and tell her himself.
But perhaps his devious mind had a reason for that, too.
Did he perhaps want her to tell the islanders? to rouse

them into making trouble so that he could have an excuse to move them over to the other side of the island, leaving him a clear field for the building of the airstrip and harbour? Tansy's mind began to whirl as she tried to put herself in his shoes, tried to work out the reasons for his actions, but it was impossible to be certain of anything when she knew only her side.

Abruptly she stood up and pulled off her shorts and shirt so that she was dressed only in a pale blue bikini. Running down to the water's edge, she plunged into the sea, swimming out into the lagoon with a clean, graceful movement that soon carried her far out past the jetty. She thought she heard a shout behind her and she turned immediately and started to swim back. It had been silly to swim out so far, there were too many hungry sharks along the coast to make swimming a safe pastime.

As she neared the shore Tansy looked to see who had called after her and then she saw Ruari jogging across the sand towards her. She ran to meet him without any embarrassment for her skimpy bikini; having played together since babyhood there wasn't much they didn't know about each other.

Tansy reached out her hands to him as he came up. 'Oh, Ruari, I've got so much to tell you! Have you heard that the soldiers have been surveying the plateau?' she asked, speaking English in her haste. 'And they used the boat to take soundings in the harbour.' Her teeth began to chatter, for the island could be cold at night after the sun went down.

'Yes, yes, I know all this,' Ruari answered. 'But you're shivering. Where are your clothes? You know you shouldn't go swimming alone, Tansy. Here, dry yourself with my shirt.' He pulled off his cotton tee-shirt and

handed it to her while they walked along to where she
had dropped her clothes.

'Yes, I know. Thank you for calling me back. I hadn't
realised I'd gone so far.'

'Called you? But I didn't, although I heard someone
shout. It was that that brought me to the beach just as
you came out of the sea.'

'It wasn't you? Then who?' Tansy frowned in puzzlement for a second, and then shrugged. 'But it doesn't
matter. What does matter, Ruari, is that Major Aston
has come to a decision on the island. He's going to ...'

'So it seems that you're not the only person on Aparoa
who speaks English, Miss Harland. Another of your little
tricks, I suppose.'

Tansy turned in surprise as a harsh voice interrupted
them, and saw Blake standing just a few yards away
under the branches of a papaya tree. They had heard no
warning of his approach and Tansy guessed that he
must be able to move as quietly as a cat, or Ruari, who
had all the inborn instinct of a man used to living by his
senses, would surely have heard him.

Ruari moved now, stepping forward and placing an
arm round Tansy's shoulders. Tansy moved nearer to
his strong protectiveness against this, her enemy, and saw
Blake's eyes narrow as he ran his eyes over her and
noted her lack of clothing. He went to make a remark,
but Ruari anticipated him.

'You are quite mistaken, Major Aston,' he said in the
excellent English he could speak when it suited him.
'Our deception in leading you to think that we spoke no
English was not Tansy's doing. She was away from the
island when you arrived. We prefer to keep strangers at
a distance and learn more of them before we decide to
extend to them the courtesy of our hospitality.'

The reproof was there, polite but explicit, and Tansy gave Ruari a little nudge of approval.

'Miss Harland, I suggest you get some clothes on before you catch cold,' Blake said, apparently ignoring Ruari's rebuff.

There was ice in Tansy's voice as she replied, 'Don't try to order me around, Major. I'm not one of your soldiers.'

He looked at her for a moment, then shrugged and turned to Ruari. 'I believe you are the headman's son. There are a great many things I would like to discuss with you and your father, and, as we can now no doubt dispense with the need of an interpreter,' (with a scathing look at Tansy) 'I suggest that I call on you tomorrow morning. If you don't want me to come to your house I will meet you wherever you wish.'

So Ruari's shot had gone home, after all, and he was unsure of his welcome in Tupuhoe's house.

'I will await you at the meeting house tomorrow, Major Aston. I teach the children there and will be holding classes for a couple of hours.'

'Very well. And now, if you're ready, Miss Harland, I'll escort you home—with or without your clothes.'

'You? You must be mad if you think I'd even walk two steps with you!'

'Nevertheless, I'm going to walk you home,' he said with a determined thrust of his chin.

Tansy didn't have to ask why. Now that he knew Ruari could speak English he wanted to tell him of his report on the island himself; would probably fill his ears with the promise of large compensations, might even think he could try to bribe Tupuhoe, as the headman, with a bigger share. Then he could add in his report of the natives' co-operation and their willingness to have the fuel base. And word it so that it would be another feather in his cap, Tansy thought with bitter irony. Turning to face Ruari, she said baldly, 'He's going to fell the whole coconut plantation to make an airstrip and he's going to blow up the mussel beds in the lagoon to deepen the harbour.'

The Major swore softly under his breath, then said savagely, 'Thank you, Miss Harland, you've now revealed yourself for what you are—interested in nothing but satisfying your own petty, selfish spite!' Then he was gone, melting into the trees as silently as he had come.

Ruari gave her her clothes and Tansy put them on, feeling nothing but misery and desolation. Slowly, haltingly, she began to tell Ruari all that had happened since she first met the Major, leaving nothing out. She knew Ruari too well to have any secrets from him. 'I started to like him, Ruari, he was witty and charming. And now—now he's done this to us.' Her voice broke on a sob.

'No, Tansy, it may not be too late.' Ruari's arm tightened comfortingly. 'Your father may still be able to do something and I will do my best to argue our case tomorrow. Perhaps it would be best if you didn't see the Major again; you're too involved now to behave rationally towards him.'

'Yes, perhaps you're right. Goodnight, Ruari.' He laid the palms of his hands against hers, as was the custom, and bade her a soft goodnight before he, too, slipped away into the darkness.

Luckily there were only a few patients at the clinic the next day, because Tansy could only concentrate with half her mind. The other half was constantly wondering how Ruari was faring in his interview with Blake Aston. She gave an injection to one patient, her legs swollen massively with elephantiasis, and could only be thankful that the disease was gradually dying out in the islands, although a cure had come too late for this poor woman.

At last she was able to go back to the house and, as the children were now freed from their lessons, gave her bag to be carried by the child who could count the highest. Ruari was waiting for her on the veranda with Tupuhoe, and Inara brought glasses of beer as soon as Tansy arrived; the natives' innate courtesy of manners would not allow them to take any refreshment in another's house without their host being present.

Tupuhoe spoke sadly in his native tongue. 'We have talked to the officer and he has shown us all on the map. He says it is most important that boats and planes should be able to come for fuel. I tell him—"Why do you not go to Papeete on Tahiti where there are already many boats and aeroplanes?", but he says this will not do. It must be in this chain of islands. He tells us the government will look after us. No one will go without food in their stomachs and clothes for their backs.' The old man looked at Tansy intently. 'But he does not think of us as men, Tansy. He does not think of our pride. I try to tell him of this through Ruari's mouth, but the officer does not understand. You must talk to him, Tansy. You are your father's daughter, but you are also a daughter of the island. You must go to the officer and tell him that we are men and must not be treated as cattle in the plantation.'

Tansy stared at the old man for a long moment, then turned questioningly to Ruari, who made a helpless gesture and said in English, 'My father is convinced that you will succeed where we have failed, because both you and the Major are British. I have tried to explain that Major Aston will not listen to you either, but he won't believe me.'

Twisting her hands together, Tansy wondered how to

tell Tupuhoe that she despised Blake Aston and never wanted to see him again, but then she looked up and saw the look of pleading in the proud old man's eyes and knew what this must mean to him. Before that, her own feelings were as nothing. She managed a small smile and said as lightly as she could, 'It might work at that. Anyway, it's worth a try.' The old man smiled too, his teeth still white and gleaming in his wrinkled face, and Ruari touched her hand gratefully.

So Tansy found herself walking up to the grey lavastone prison building the following afternoon, after having racked her brains for something to say to the Major that would persuade him to leave them in peace. A soldier was cleaning some equipment near the massive doors of the gallows gate, but he sprang up as Tansy approached, looking her over appreciatively as she stood slim and straight in a cheese-cloth blouse and cotton skirt.

'I'd like to speak to Major Aston, please,' she said formally.

'Yes, miss. If you'll follow me, I'll take you to him.'

He led the way across the courtyard, the high walls, topped with metal spikes, plunging all but one corner in deepest shade, and then up two flights of stairs to the old council chamber. This was a large room, sparsely furnished with an old table and a cupboard built into the wall, but it had been changed from the dusty room that Tansy remembered into an office. Maps and charts were pinned to the walls and papers were spread out on the table where John Andrews sat busily pounding a typewriter. Blake Aston was standing with his back to her, making some annotations on a partly finished, large scale chart of the lagoon, but he turned as the soldier opened the door and then straightened up abruptly when he saw Tansy behind him. John, too, stood up as she entered.

'Miss Harland.' Blake's voice was devoid of expression.

Tansy clenched her fists; this was going to be even harder than she had supposed. 'I—I should like to speak to you, please.'

Time seemed to stand still as he looked at her steadily for a long moment, then he said, 'Very well. John, would you mind?'

Tansy heard a chair scrape, the door close, and then they were alone.

'Well, Miss Harland?' His tone was as hard as his face.

'Th-there's something I'd like to show you.'

'Look, if this is some trick to try and persuade me to alter my report, then you're wasting your time.'

Leaning forward to grip the edge of the table, Tansy said intensely, 'You're threatening to take everything we have away from us. You owe us the right to do everything in our power to put our case.'

His grey eyes looked at her speculatively and saw the effort this was costing her. 'All right, I grant you that. What is it you want to show me?'

'It's quite a long way from here. It would be quickest in the jeep.'

'I'll have the driver bring it round.'

'No, please.' Tansy reached out to touch his sleeve as he walked past her, then hastily drew her hand away. His mouth tightened as he noticed her quick withdrawal. 'Just you.'

He raised an eyebrow quizzically. 'Have I your word that this isn't just another trick?'

Tansy nodded, not trusting herself to speak. Too much was at stake for her to lose her temper now.

'Then we'd better get started.'

Soon Blake was driving them along the coastal road, sometimes so close to the sea that the ocean spray spumed across the road and engulfed them in a million rainbows. Tansy directed him up a narrow inland track, but after about half a mile this petered out and he drew to a stop, looking at her questioningly.

'We have to walk from here,' Tansy explained. 'The path follows the river for a little way and then branches off.'

They began to climb along the path that wound gradually uphill alongside the tumbling river into undergrowth that became more wild and dense. Rain came suddenly, a tropical shower, warm and heavy, strong with the scents of the jungle across the river. They took what cover they could beneath the spreading branches of a tree, but soon they were both soaked to the skin, their clothes clinging to them. As soon as the rain stopped Tansy moved out on to the path again, the intense heat of the sun drying them almost as quickly as the rain had wet them.

Tansy didn't try to talk to Blake as they went along; she didn't want to get drawn into any arguments which might prejudice what she had in mind. The river had become much shallower now and they were able to ford it and enter the jungle on the other side. Here great trees, strangling beneath twisting lianas and with vine-ropes woven between them, fought the sun, trying to keep it out of their domain. Stray birds, distant and alone, flew through the trees, darting from one shaft of light to another. The dim haze of the gloomy daytime seemed like twilight here and they could see no more than a few feet into the dense growth on either side of the path. No breath of air moved, making the atmosphere oppressive and forbidding, but there was a sweet, heavy scent which hung everywhere; the odour of the jungle, which had a slightly aphrodisiac quality, a fact which the natives learned long ago.

At last they came to the end of their climb and emerged at the end of the coconut plantation furthest from the sea where cacao trees grew haphazardly to form a barrier between plantation and jungle. Here, deep in the grove, Tansy led Blake to a small house that would have been impossible to find for anyone who didn't know the way.

'What is this place? Who lives here?' Blake asked sharply.

'You'll see in a moment. It's all right, they know you're coming. You will be welcome.'

Blake looked at her keenly, then nodded and followed her towards the native hut, a building with a solid teak-wood base and a roof of heavy thatch with walls of woven coconut palm. The walls were built in two halves, the upper halves being propped open to let what slight breeze there was cool the interior. A boy of about ten saw them coming and called to someone inside. In answer to the call a man came to the door. His hair was white, his face deeply lined from years of constant pain, the reason for which became clear as he limped out to greet them and they saw that his body was misshapen and twisted. Nevertheless, there was a singularly warm smile in his eyes as he came courteously to greet them.

'Tansy. Major Aston, you are welcome in my house.' Although a native he spoke very good, if heavily accented English. He motioned them to precede him inside and here a native woman shyly indicated the pandanus mats spread on the floor for them to sit on. Tansy immediately sank gracefully down and, after a moment's hesitation, Blake joined her.

'My name is Damaru,' the native told Blake as he sat

opposite them. 'And this is my wife, Yaka, and my son, Dakua. You will eat and drink with us.' The words were more a command than an invitation and soon Yaka had brought them coconut cups of toddy and bowls of raw fish dipped in salt water and coconut sauce. Tansy smiled at Yaka and thanked her in Polynesian, for the woman spoke no English.

'We live very simply, Major,' Damaru began. 'But it is because I choose to do so. The coconut trees and the jungle provide us with most of our food and materials for our shelter, and the cacao seeds we barter to furnish our other needs. We saw you when you and your men were measuring the plateau, but you did not see us, I think.'

'No,' Blake admitted. 'I had no idea this house was here.'

'And if the airstrip is built here, Major? What will become of us?'

Blake's jaw tightened. 'The runway won't come as far as this, but I have to tell you that this area may have to be cleared in case our planes overshoot.'

'I understand.' Damaru looked steadily at Blake, but the Major returned his look without flinching, his face completely impassive, nothing of what he must be thinking betrayed in his face. Tansy sat with the native woman and the boy and silently watched the two men; so different, and yet in some way the same, for they both had extremely strong characters.

'I will tell you a story, Major Aston,' Damaru said softly. 'A story of war. Once there was a young boy of nine summers, of Dakua's age.' He pointed to the boy who smiled at the sound of his name. 'This boy lived on an island many hundreds of miles from here. Soldiers of a far country came there and they made the people give them food and shelter. Then other soldiers, who were fighting the first, came and tortured the boy's father, the headman of the village, until he told them where the first soldiers were hiding. When they found out they killed him. But some of the first soldiers escaped and they came seeking revenge. The father was dead, so they tortured his son instead and left him to die. But the boy survived and he swore that he would go to a place where no soldiers, no matter of what nation—for all soldiers are of the same breed—would ever come to. So when he became old enough he travelled many miles and visited many lands until he found a place where he and his family would be safe for the rest of their lives.' Then, abruptly, he said, 'How old do you think I am, Major? Please tell me truly.'

Surprised, Blake looked at his white head and said, 'Between sixty or seventy, I should think.'

'No, Major, I am not yet fifty years old. I was the young boy, and the island on which I lived was called Guadalcanal.' With great dignity he spread his hands to indicate the grove around them. 'Major Aston, if you take this away, where in the world can I go to escape your kind?'

He began to get slowly, painfully to his feet and Blake automatically rose to help him, but Damaru ignored his outstretched hand and managed alone. Blake immediately turned sharply and walked out of the house.

After a quick word of goodbye, Tansy hurried after him, afraid that he might get lost if he tried to traverse the jungle alone. But he was waiting for her in the cacao grove out of sight of the house, a look of savage fury on his face. Tansy stopped precipitately and stared at him. Above them a flock of birds, green, red, purple and yellow lorikeets swirled and eddied through the grove,

their cries harsh in the still air. The shimmering, iridescent leaves of the cacao bushes, shading from brightest
vermilion to deep red and from pale green to purple or
yellow, made the grove one of the loveliest places on
Aparoa, but Tansy had eyes for nothing but her enemy
standing so menacingly before her. And she knew that
she had failed. Damaru's pitiful story had meant nothing
to him.

'I thought you said you weren't going to pull any
tricks!' he said furiously.

'It wasn't a trick. I wanted you to see what . . .'

'I know what you wanted to do,' he interjected before
she could finish. 'You wanted to play on my sympathy to
try to get me to change my mind. Well, it won't work!'

'No, I should have known that with you it wouldn't.
You're too heartless to care about anyone else,' Tansy
retorted, the fragile hold on her temper shattered.

'My God, Tansy, do you think I won't have that man
and his family—this whole island—on my conscience
for the rest of my life?'

He had called her by her christian name for the first
time, but Tansy was too blazingly angry to notice. 'Conscience?' she jibed. 'I don't believe you have one. I think
you care about nothing but yourself and your career. If
you had any real feelings for these people then you could
easily alter your report, tell NATO that Aparoa wouldn't
be any use to them.'

Contemptuously he said, 'You want me to lie to my
superiors?'

'I'd rather have a lie on my conscience than the desecration of a whole island!' Tansy said tensely. Then,
when he remained silent, she went on quickly, 'These
people have always been independent of others. They're
a very proud race. Slowly, they are beginning to accept

progress and learning to cope with it while still maintaining their old traditions. One of these is that they provide for their own. If you build them new houses, give them clothes and food and all the other things they need because the men are unable to do so, then you will take away their human dignity; they won't be able to lift up their heads as men any more.' She stopped and looked up at Blake with desperate appeal in her eyes.

He continued to look down at her for a full minute and for a few breathless heartbeats she thought that she had won, after all. But then, 'No, Tansy,' he said on what could have been a sigh. 'This decision is too crucial for that. If you hadn't spent your whole life cooped up in this remote place you would have been able to work that out for yourself. Don't you ever read a paper or listen to the radio? The eastern bloc countries have stepped up their armaments programmes; it's vital that we have a base in this area.' He reached out and took hold of her arms, shaking her gently as he tried to make her see his viewpoint. 'Can't you understand? It's to prevent anything like Guadalcanal ever happening again that we must be strong. Only by being as strong as them will we prevent another war. Don't you see that?'

'No! If there weren't any soldiers there wouldn't be any wars!'

'If one country has them then we all must,' he said impatiently.

'And does that mean that you have to be part of it? I hate everything that you stand for, Major Aston—war, violence, the principle that you can only fight force with force; and I despise anyone who is weak enough to live by those tenets!' Tansy was past caring now, she wanted to hurt him as much as he had hurt her.

'You little fool! You don't know what you're talking

about.' He shook her again, angrily now. 'You live in this backwater and you think you can preach to the rest of the world. If you want to help these people why don't you do something useful? Learn how to be a teacher in the school or something, instead of running around in that damn sarong pretending to be a native girl. You say you despise me for what I am; have you ever thought that wasting your life is equally despicable?' he said harshly.

Tansy stared at him incredulously, then, rage overcoming her, she lifted her hand and struck him as hard as she could across the face. He jerked his head back, his jaw tense. He let go of her and, very deliberately, raised his hand and hit her in return. Not a hard blow or he would certainly have knocked her down, but a stinging slap with his cupped hand that brought stars to her eyes. For a second she swayed, as much with shock as with pain, then opened her eyes to find Blake glaring down at her.

'I'm a soldier, remember?' he said bitingly. 'When someone hits me I hit back.'

Without a word Tansy turned and ran unseeingly from the grove and into the jungle. Whether Blake was following her or not she didn't stop to look. Let him get lost for all she cared! She only wanted to get away from the man who was so alien to anyone she had ever known before, away from all the things he stood for. She came at last to where the jeep stood in the shade of some giant ferns and went to run past it and continue along the track on foot, but, before she had gone more than ten yards, a strong arm caught her and pulled her to a stop.

'Get in the jeep. I'll drive you home.'

'I'm not going anywhere with you!' Tansy shouted at him.

'Stop behaving like a sulky child. I brought you and I'm taking you back.'

'Go to hell!' Tansy tried to prise his fingers from her arm, but the next moment found herself picked up and thrown over his broad shoulder. Frenziedly she beat at him with her clenched fists and tried to kick him, but he dumped her in the passenger seat of the jeep and held her there while he climbed in.

'You little wildcat,' he muttered angrily as she clawed at him. 'For someone who hates violence you really fight dirty, lady.' He kept a tight hold of her wrist until they were driving along too fast for her to jump out.

'You great bully! You're loathsome, do you know that? As loathsome as the job you came here to do. You're just the type to use brute force to get your own way!'

Blake's jaw was set in a hard line as he said savagely, 'Don't push me too far, lady, or one of these days I might do just that!'

Tansy couldn't get out of the jeep fast enough when at last he pulled up outside her house in a swirl of dust. She was about to run up the path when she saw that old Amaru, the woman who kept her pigs in the prison court-yard, was sitting patiently waiting for her. Reluctantly she stopped. 'What is it, Amaru? Are you ill?' she asked in the island dialect.

'No, girl, I am well. It is the soldiers. They want to buy two of my pigs. Shall I sell to them?' The old native woman pointed to Blake as she mentioned the soldiers. He had been about to drive off until he noticed the gesture, but then stopped to see if their talk concerned him.

Tansy looked at him, sitting so implacably in the jeep. She shook her head decisively at Amaru. 'No, do not sell them your pigs. Tell everyone in the village, and tell them to spread the word to all their relations on the island; no one is to sell anything to the soldiers. No animals, or crops, or even fruit from the trees. Nothing! We did not ask them to come here. They must provide for themselves.'

Blake could not have understood a word of their conversation, but he got the implication all right. He shot Tansy a look of cold rage that made her feel as if he had struck her again, then he accelerated and drove away fast up the hill.

Once inside the house and in her room, Tansy examined her face in the mirror. The marks of his fingers could still be plainly seen on her cheek. She stared at her reflection for a long time, trying to come to terms with the violent emotions that the man had aroused in her. Never before had her passions been so provoked that she had struck someone. It was against every principle she upheld. And, she thought ironically, she had been proved right, for violence had begat violence; the mark of it was on her face! Why had she so lost control of herself? Blake had hurt her when he had accused her of going native, of wasting her life, but she could simply have told him that he was wrong, that she was a doctor. But it had been his ready assumption that she was just a lotus-eater that had hurt, she admitted to herself. He hadn't even bothered to wonder what she did when she wasn't acting as interpreter for him, just took it for granted that she lazed around and gossiped like the native women. Inevitably she began to wonder *why* it had hurt so much, but she pushed the thought quickly to the back of her mind. Blake Aston was different from any other man she had ever met, had excited emotions that she didn't know she could feel, and for her own peace of mind it would be better to keep her thoughts and her person as far away from him as possible. Decisively Tansy sent Inara to tell her four native rowers to get the sailing canoe ready—it was time she visited some of the outlying islands.

It was while she was in the clinic collecting some drugs to take with her that Ruari came to find her. One swift glance at her set face and he knew that her mission had failed. Typically he didn't bother to ask for explanations.

'How long will you be away?'

'About three or four days, I should think.'

'You have told everyone not to sell them food. Is that wise, Tansy?' he asked gently.

'We don't want them here. Why should we feed them? Anyway, they'll probably be leaving very soon so that the Major can submit his report.'

'No, he told me that he would be sending his findings over the radio and he is to remain here until a decision is made. Then, if Aparoa is chosen, he and his men will start clearing the plateau and blasting the harbour straight away.'

Tansy turned and looked at him, a box of drugs in her hand. So by going away she wouldn't have seen the last of Blake after all. For it was a foregone conclusion that Aparoa would be selected; she had spent hours poring over her father's maps of the other two islands and could see even from those that they wouldn't be as suitable as Aparoa. She shrugged; what did it matter? It would be easy enough to keep well out of his way, and he certainly wouldn't be seeking her out again.

'Well, they'll just have to eat the rations they brought with them, won't they,' she told Ruari callously, adding, 'By the way, don't tell him I'm a doctor, will you? Let him think that Daddy is the only one on the island.'

Ruari studied her thoughtfully. 'What is between you and Major Aston, Tansy?'

'Nothing!' Tansy replied vehemently as she dropped the drugs into her bag. 'Absolutely nothing!'

# CHAPTER FOUR

IT was five days before Tansy returned to Aparoa, her journey delayed by a storm. Five days in which she had done her best to forget what might be happening to her beloved island and of the man who was awaiting orders to ravage it. But when they paddled through the gap in the coral and entered the lagoon all looked the same as before; the coconut palms on the plateau nodded their heads gracefully towards the ocean, children played and swam at the river's mouth. For a moment her heart lifted, but then she saw the army boat tied up at the old jetty and knew that the soldiers were still there.

Ruari was waiting to meet her and lifted her from the canoe to the shore. The sadness in his bleak face told Tansy that all hope had been in vain.

'When?' she asked him in little more than a whisper.

'Major Aston received confirmation that Aparoa had been chosen only this morning. It seems that your father had some influence after all, and his friends put up many arguments against using the island, but they weren't strong enough. Come, you are just in time. Everyone has been called to the meeting house. The Major says that he will tell the villagers himself and he wants me to translate.'

Already there was a mass of people waiting in the cleared space outside the meeting house, but, for Aparoa, it was a silent crowd. Gone was the usual shouting and laughing, the jokes and the cheerful badinage. Instead they talked quietly among themselves, murmuring, conjecturing, knowing that their lives were going to be changed but not really believing it, hoping against hope that all would be as it had always been. Tansy stayed at the back of the crowd, shaking her head when Ruari went to draw her into the meeting house with him. He didn't press her and soon he, Tupuhoe and Blake came out on to the veranda to face the villagers.

Blake's face was completely impassive as he told them all exactly what he was going to do. He explained that a government official would come and work out adequate compensation for everyone who had lost their land or their livelihood. His voice was strong and clear, as if he was merely addressing his men instead of ruining a way of life that had been in existence for a thousand years. His eyes swept the crowd and came to rest on Tansy, her silver-blonde hair making her immediately noticeable. Did his voice falter for just a second? If it did he recovered so quickly that it was impossible to say with any certainty.

Carefully Ruari interpreted his every word until the end. There was a moment of silence, every face turned up to him, expecting more, and there was so little to give. Some began to ask questions. When would the work start?

'Tomorrow,' Blake replied. 'And every day until the job is done.'

Many muttered resentfully, but others said, '*Aita Peapea.* It doesn't matter. We can do nothing,' and gathered round Tupuhoe, who comforted his people as best he could while Ruari went with Blake in the jeep to repeat the message in all the other villages on the island.

Tansy took her clinic and later in the afternoon got out the pony and trap to visit her bedridden patients. Everywhere there was the same dismay and hopelessness, for the plantation was the whole island's source of a cash crop. Unhappy faces looked into hers, begged her for reassurance, but Tansy had none to give; her heart was as heavy as theirs.

That night she went to Tupuhoe's house and stayed there for a long time trying to plan what was best to be done; where was the best place for a new plantation to be cleared and planted; could the mussels be transferred further down the bay; where could they find enough grazing for the cattle? They talked for hours and it had been dark for some time before Tansy left the men still talking. Dressed in her sarong and with a flower in her hair, she walked along deep in thought. Then, without warning, a man stepped out from the trees ahead of her, a dark shadow, but not dark enough for her not to see that the man was in army uniform. For a second she thought it was Blake, but the man, although tall, wasn't tall enough.

'What do you want?' she asked sharply.

'Oh, it's not a question of what I want, darlin',' the soldier said with a cockney twang to his voice, 'it's what I'm going to give to you.' As he reached out for her Tansy turned instinctively to run, but he was swift on his feet and caught her easily, turning her round to face him and pulling her close to him.

'Come on, darlin'. I only want a few kisses. The other blokes go for the native girls, but they don't turn me on, not like you do. And you wouldn't go around dressed like that if you weren't hot for it.' He had been drinking and Tansy could taste the stench of beer on his breath as he pressed his lips against hers, his stubbly chin scraping her skin as she struggled to get free.

She scratched his face and he swore at her, then deliberately tripped her so that she fell to the ground with him on top of her. Desperately Tansy tried to yell for help, but he covered her mouth with one hand while with the other he tried to pull the sarong from her writhing body. Tansy bit his hand as hard as she could, ready to scream as soon as she drew away. But suddenly his weight was pulled off her, she heard the sound of some heavy blows landing on flesh and scrambled to her feet in time to see Blake Aston landing a blow to the soldier's jaw that sent him crashing senseless to the ground.

Tansy could only stand and stare as Blake stood over the fallen man, then she became aware that the sarong had fallen off and she turned with trembling fingers to retrieve it and put it on. Her hands were shaking so much that she couldn't tie it properly and Blake came silently to do it for her. She looked up at him, tried to say something, but found that she couldn't speak.

'I told you not to wear that damned thing!' he said savagely, and then she was held in the warm safety of his arms as she burst into tears and cried out her shock and terror on his shoulder.

At last her sobs steadied and she became aware that he was gently stroking her hair. 'I'm—I'm all right now, thank you,' she managed.

He smiled at her politeness. 'You'd better come and sit down for a while. Here.' He offered her his handkerchief as he led her to a fallen treetrunk.

'What about the soldier?' Tansy asked hesitantly. 'Is he badly hurt?'

Blake glanced back at where the man still lay stretched out on the ground. 'No, he'll be all right. I'll deal with him in the morning when he's had time to sober up.'

'You won't—you won't court-martial him or anything?'

'Not unless you bring a charge.'

'What will you do with him?'

'Confine him to the prison building, give him all the worst jobs to do until we leave. That should dampen his ardour for a bit. Feeling better now?'

'Yes, thank you.' Tansy had become acutely aware that only a moment ago she had been held in his arms, even if it was only to comfort her. 'I'm afraid I made your shirt wet.'

He grinned, a slightly crooked grin, that Tansy had never seen on his face before. For a moment it made him look somehow boyish, and infinitely attractive. She suddenly remembered how much she hated him.

'I'd better get home. I'll have the handkerchief sent up to you tomorrow.'

She rose to go, but he put out a hand to stop her. 'Wait, Tansy, I want to talk to you.'

'What is it?' She had stopped, but stood with her back to him making no effort to rejoin him on the treetrunk.

'You know you shouldn't be out alone, don't you? And I told you not to wear that sarong. The soldier was at fault, but you put plenty of temptation in his way.' There was a rough edge to his voice.

Tansy turned and stared at him. 'Are you trying to tell me that it's dangerous for me to be out alone at night? Have you so little control over your men that the island women aren't safe any more? We were perfectly safe before you came. No native would attack a woman!' she said bitterly.

He stood up and came to stand beside her, any gentleness disappearing completely from his manner. 'I can't confine all the men for the whole of the time they're not working. And if you go flaunting yourself ...'

'I don't *flaunt* myself!' Tansy interrupted indignantly, then added caustically, 'And just what were you doing out here tonight anyway, Major Aston? Have the tropics got to you, too? Were you looking for a native girl to amuse yourself with? Well, you shouldn't have too hard a search; the people on Aparoa don't suffer from civilised sexual repressions, they're open and candid about it. But they don't go creeping around in the dark, or forcing themselves on someone who doesn't want them. They just have to ask, and if the answer's yes, they go off into the jungle and make love!'

'And is that what you were doing when I caught you on the beach with your native boy-friend?' Blake cut in, his eyes blazing.

Tansy looked up at him in consternation. 'Ruari isn't my boy-friend. We were brought up together.'

'Isn't he?' Blake stared grimly in the moonlight. 'Maybe you'd better try telling him that. It certainly seemed like it from the way he held you and looked at you that night!'

Shaking her head in incredulous repugnance, Tansy started to back away from him as she would from something dirty. 'You're disgusting, and you have a vile mind. You may be an officer, but you're certainly not a gentleman!'

'I don't *feel* like a gentleman—not as far as you're concerned.'

'And you certainly don't act like one! Or you wouldn't have hit me like you did.'

There were steely glints in his dark eyes as he glowered down at her. 'No, I don't, do I? Would you rather I'd done this?' He pulled her roughly into his arms and kissed her with such intensity that her lips parted beneath the pressure of his mouth. He held her closer until her body fitted into the hard curve of his and for a few breathless seconds Tansy was too overwhelmed to resist him, but as she came to her senses she started to struggle wildly. Immediately he let her go and stepped back.

Raising her hand to her bruised lips, Tansy said slowly, 'Why did you do that?'

'Because you went too far this time, and because I'm just a common soldier, isn't that what you think me? Did you expect something better of me?' he jeered at her derisively.

'No. No, I didn't. You're no better than he is,' Tansy said, pointing to the man who was beginning to stir on the ground. Then she turned and ran towards the comforting safety of her own home.

Soon after dawn the next morning the island was a hive of unusual activity as the natives busily rescued what they could before the destruction began, while the soldiers were out with their equipment, pegging the site to be cleared. The road to the plateau was thronged with horses and wagons, trailers towed by bicycles and even hand-pulled carts as everyone collected the coconuts and took them down to the villages to be stored. Sometimes the jeep's horn would blare as the natives took their time in moving to make way for it to pass, and more than once a confrontation between soldier and hot-headed native as one got in the way of the other was only prevented by the intervention of one of the officers or by Ruari and Tupuhoe. Towards noon a large ship appeared on the horizon and anchored in the bay, outside the coral reef. Everyone who was not working immediately went down to the beach to watch the smaller army boat ferry equipment from the ship to the island, the explosives and detonators being brought carefully ashore first and stored in the dark cellars of the old prison.

The activity went on until dusk, but Tansy was not

there to see it; she had gone to the other side of the island and stayed there all day, not returning until the harbour was again silent and the people returned to their homes to cook their meals. That evening she asked Inara to sleep at the house and the native woman readily agreed without asking why. For some things no questions were necessary.

Realising that this might be one of the last times that she was able to do so, Tansy put on a sweater and jeans and went up to her special place at the edge of the plantation. But even here she could not escape from the harshness of reality, for the big ship still lay at anchor in the bay, its lights reflected in the tranquil waters. Tansy wondered if Blake had asked for fresh food supplies to be brought for them; his men must be heartily sick of army rations by now, she thought with some satisfaction. Restlessly she turned her back on the ship and went to wander a little way along the path through the plantation. The gentle breeze set the fronds of the palms swaying like a dancer's skirts, but Tansy shivered suddenly. The attack by the soldier the previous night must have unnerved her, for she felt constantly as if she was being watched. Even the pleasure of this small nightly ritual had been taken from her, and she turned and hurried to the house where Inara was waiting for her.

The unloading continued all the next day, most of the time being taken up with the precarious task of manoeuvring a bulldozer on to a raft and pulling it slowly through the sea and towards the gap in the reef. Everyone stopped what they were doing to watch this tricky operation, and even Tansy stood at the window of the clinic and held her breath while she watched Blake himself take the wheel of the boat. He waited to gauge the exact time to take the raft through on the swell of a wave without having it come crashing down on to the boat if it came too fast. Eventually it was safely through and headed towards the beach where the raft could be driven ashore and the bulldozer rolled off. The supply ship didn't wait to see the end of the operation but gave a farewell hoot before turning to speed away to the west.

Tansy, too, didn't stay to watch the end because she had arranged to speak to her father on the radio that afternoon and went back to the house to the transmitter kept in his den. Putting on the headphones, she expertly tuned in to the correct wavelength and was soon in touch with David Harland, who was still in Canberra. Air time was limited, so Tansy found herself hastily telling her father all that was happening on the island, while he in turn told her of his hopes that his friends' influence would succeed, how he had tried to persuade the NATO representatives to survey more islands, but of their refusal because of lack of time.

'Will you be coming home now, Daddy?' Tansy asked eagerly.

'I don't know.' There was hesitation in David Harland's voice. 'I thought of staying on here for two or three more weeks. I could do with a break after all the running around I've been doing in Australia.'

'But, Daddy,' Tansy's voice was filled with dismay, 'we need ...' She was about to go on to tell him how much the islanders needed him on Aparoa at the moment, when a young native boy burst into the room and pulled wildly at her arm, shouting something she couldn't hear.

'Wait a minute.'

Taking off the earphones, she was able to hear him say excitedly, 'Come quick, Tansy! The bulldozer slipped and fell on a soldier. It was the officer. You must come quick.'

Appalled, Tansy whispered, 'Which officer?'

'The young one. The lieutenant who collects the shells.'

Tansy quickly spoke to her father. 'Daddy, I have to go, there's been an accident.' Then she had grabbed her bag and was running as hard as she could towards the beach.

When she arrived there the crowd immediately parted for her and she found that they had already freed John Andrews from under the machine by digging the sand from underneath him, and that Blake was leaning over him examining his injuries. Tansy pushed a burly sergeant who tried to hold her back out of the way and dropped down on her knees on the other side of John's prostrate body.

Blake glanced up and then tried to keep the sight of the wounds from her. 'What the hell are you doing here? This is no place for you. I don't want fainting women on my hands.'

Without bothering to reply, Tansy brushed his arm aside and saw that the bulldozer must have trapped John's right leg. Already Blake had applied a tourniquet, but after a swift inspection Tansy could see that there were deep gashes on his upper leg and the ankle bone was broken. Completely ignoring Blake, she turned to two of the natives and told them in their own tongue to run to the clinic and bring a stretcher, and another she told to warn Inara to prepare the small operating theatre.

'I've told them to take John to the clinic,' she told Blake. 'The cuts will need stitching and the bone re-setting.'

'I'll send a radio message to the supply ship and get them to turn back. They can take him to the nearest hospital.'

'That won't be necessary. I can treat him here,' Tansy said calmly.

'You?' His voice was scathing. 'If you think I'm going to let you play around with that boy's leg, you're crazy!'

'Oh, don't be so ridiculous! Open your eyes, Major,' Tansy retorted. 'Who do you think looks after the islanders while my father's away?'

'All right, so maybe he's taught you a thing or two, but you're still a rank amateur, Miss Harland, and I ...'

'No, Major,' she cut in icily as she reached for her bag, 'I'm not an amateur. I'm a qualified doctor and as much a professional as you are.'

She would have liked to have seen the expression that remark brought to his face, but John began to stir just then and she had to administer a pain-killing drug that sent him back into oblivion. The two men came with the stretcher and she supervised her patient's transfer to the clinic, Blake making no move now to hinder her. Tansy left him to finish unloading his precious bulldozer while she prepared for the emergency operation. Inara was always her helper on these occasions when David Harland was away, and Tansy experienced no undue difficulties, although the operation was a rather long and delicate one as she had to carefully remove minute splinters of bone from the crushed foot. At last the wounds were stitched and dressed, the foot in plaster, and John wheeled out of the theatre into an empty side-room.

Rubbing her neck rather wearily, Tansy removed her mask and pulled off the surgical cap as she walked into the small office. Blake rose as she entered and she wondered how long·he had been waiting there.

'How is he?' he asked.

'He'll do. Although he won't be able to walk on that foot for quite some time. He was very lucky, the soft sand underneath him acted like a cushion—otherwise his foot would have been completely shattered.'

'Do you have accommodation for him here?'

'It will be best if he stays here for a few days until I'm quite sure he's got over the operation safely, then we can make other arrangements. Inara and I will take care of him. He should come round in an hour or two—you can come back and see him then, if you like.'

'Thank you, I'll do that.' But he made no move to leave.

'Don't let me keep you, Major. I know how busy you must be,' Tansy said sarcastically as she reached behind her to undo the tapes of her theatre gown.

'Let me help you.'

He raised a hand to untie the bow, but Tansy stepped quickly away. 'I can manage, thanks.' And she took off the gown.

'So you can,' Blake said softly, and suddenly the room was filled with an electric tension. Tansy didn't look at him, instead going to sit at her father's desk to write up her report of the operation. 'Why didn't you tell me?'

She didn't have to ask what he was talking about. 'I don't have to justify myself to you, Major,' she countered.

He studied her for a moment, his eyes hard. 'No, you don't.' Then, abruptly, 'Where did you train?'

'In London. My diploma's on the wall if you don't believe me.'

'Oh, I believe you. I just wanted to see how far you'd gone in this new little game you're playing.'

'Game?' Tansy stared at him.

'Well, isn't it a game? You could have told me who and what you were from the outset, in which case I would have treated you as an adult woman; but you chose to play at being a native girl. And you thoroughly enjoyed yourself back there on the beach when you tried to give me my come-uppance, didn't you?'

'That isn't true,' Tansy exclaimed indignantly. 'If John hadn't been hurt you would probably never have known I was a doctor.'

'Oh, I think you would have found a way of letting me know. You're pretty good at manipulating things the way you want them on this island. Even before we came here you were determined to make things as unpleasant as possible for us by rousing up the natives to obstruct us as much as they could by pretending not to understand English. I know Ruari said it wasn't your fault, but I bet you let them know you thought it would be a hell of a good idea,' he added as Tansy opened her mouth to protest. 'Ruari isn't the only one who speaks English, either, as I found out when I went round the villages the other day. A great many of them forgot they were supposed to be ignorant savages and asked questions about our plans. But you deliberately chose to keep me in the dark.'

His voice was tense, his eyes dark with contempt as he went on, 'And now you've given the islanders instructions not to sell us any food. You even had the temerity to do it in front of my face! And as a doctor you must know that we need fresh fruit and vegetables to keep fit in the tropics. Ever since we came here you've acted like a spoilt, wilful child whose favourite toy has been taken away from you. You've incited the islanders to hate us and turned what could have been a peaceable mission into one which could erupt into a dangerous situation at any moment. Already today there have been two or three incidents between the natives and my men which could have become nasty if they hadn't been nipped in the bud at the outset.' He stopped for a second and looked down at Tansy where she sat, white-faced, behind the desk. 'I'm giving you one last chance, *Dr* Harland—stop acting like a child and start behaving like a sensible adult. You've proved that you've got a brain—use it! Tell the natives they won't lose by our coming here and let them sell us their produce. I could even use some of them to help us in our work.'

Tansy looked at him, her temper for once held in check. 'Is that an order, Major?' she asked with deceptive calmness.

Blake raised one eyebrow slightly as a wary look came into his eyes. 'If you want to take it that way.'

'And when would you like me to start—how shall I put it—co-operating with the enemy?'

'This isn't a war, Tansy,' he said softly.

'Isn't it?' She rose now to face him. 'What else would you call it when a group of men—foreigners—come and take over your country, seize your property and take away your livelihood? Even use you to help desecrate your own lands; just like you used me when you first came here,' she said bitterly.

'You needn't have helped us. You had a choice.'

'No, Major, you took away my right to choose when you made me afraid for the islanders. You used my feelings for them to make me do what you wanted, and you know it. Well, it's very condescending of you, Major Aston, but you won't find any fifth columnists on Aparoa!'

'You're being ridiculous.' His voice had an edge to it now and Tansy could see a small pulse beat in his temple just where a short curl of dark hair protruded from his beret. 'This whole operation could be of benefit to everyone if it could just be conducted in a peaceful manner and ...'

'Oh, you'd like that, wouldn't you?' Tansy broke in derisively. 'How you'd love to have us all running around to your bidding! But it isn't going to be that way. I was against war until I met you, but now I'm beginning to see that it's the only language you understand, so from now on you're going to have to fight every step of the way!'

Blake leant to place his hands on the desk which brought his angry eyes down level with hers. 'Don't fight me, Tansy,' he said softly. There was a threat in his voice, but was there also the smallest note of pleading? Tansy's eyes stared into his and she found that her heart was beating painfully in her chest. 'You can't win and you're only going to get hurt in the process.'

At that Tansy's head came up and her chin jutted defiantly. 'Don't be so damn sure of yourself, Major. You may just have the unique experience of losing a fight!'

Blake straightened up, his face as black as thunder. Then he turned precipitately and strode out of the room.

Tansy sank down into the chair again, the battle of words leaving her feeling weak and drained. It gradually dawned on her that she had committed the whole island to a sort of guerilla war and for a moment she was appalled at what she had done. Then indignation came pouring back. How dared he come and start to preach at her? Blake might only be acting on instructions from above, but as the representative of the faceless THEM who issued the orders, he would have to be the one to take the consequences. No government on earth should have the power to take away a man's right to live where and how he wanted. Tansy determined there and then that Aparoa's objections were going to make themselves felt!

# CHAPTER FIVE

WHEN John Andrews recovered consciousness Tansy was sitting at his bedside, ready to comfort and reassure him. With light fingers she took his pulse and told him quietly where he was. He cheered up a bit when he learnt that he had suffered no permanent injuries, but groaned when Tansy told him it could be months before he would be completely recovered.

'Oh, lord, I suppose that means they'll ship me back to England and I'll get posted away from Blake's command,' he said ruefully.

'Would that matter so much?' Tansy asked as she helped him to sip some water.

'I'll say it would. Blake isn't like some of the other senior officers; he really shows you how to go about things and helps you to get on. I was jolly lucky to get sent here with him. Not that Aparoa's anything like I expected,' he admitted as he sank back against the pillows again.

'Oh? What did you expect?' Tansy encouraged him to talk, pleased that he seemed to have come out of the operation so well.

He grinned rather shamefacedly. 'Well, I suppose I expected it to be rather like the films. You know, dusky maidens in grass skirts doing the hula-hula while we sat around feasting under the stars. But instead everyone has kept out of our way, except the kids. The adults just watch us sullenly and won't speak to us—and as for the dusky maidens, they run a mile if we even smile at them.'

Tansy laughed at him and told him to rest. 'Go to sleep and dream about your hula-hula dancers,' she advised him.

John grinned and looked up at her. 'You're a nurse or doctor, aren't you?'

'Now how did you guess that?'

'You took my pulse so professionally, and besides, you've got very bossy. Women always get bossy when they've got a man helpless.'

'Why, Lieutenant Andrews, I had no idea you were such a man of the world,' she said in mock amazement. 'Now go to sleep.'

'See!' he said with smug satisfaction.

Inara was waiting to sit with John through the evening and Tansy told her that Blake could go in to see him if he came. She herself went home to rest for a few hours before returning to spend the night at the clinic. Inara said that Blake had called with John's belongings, but that John had still been asleep and so he hadn't disturbed him. When John woke again the anaesthetic affected him and he felt ill and nauseous. Tansy gave him an injection to relieve the symptoms and settled him down for the night before carrying in a chair for herself and plugging in a reading lamp.

For a couple of hours she caught up on various medical journals, occasionally making notes in a small notebook; there were one or two articles on tropical diseases that she found particularly interesting and wanted to follow up. Several times John stirred restlessly, the dressings on his legs and the heavy plaster on his foot making him hot and uncomfortable. An electric fan helped to cool the air of the hot, still night a little, but Tansy went to the open window to get what little breeze there was from the sea.

She felt a strange sense of frustration, a feeling that was alien to her nature, for she was generally contented with her life. But tonight she felt the need of something she couldn't define. The great silver disc of the full moon, surrounded by its satellites of distant stars, seemed to smile mockingly down at her. She longed for something, but didn't know what it was. Then the remembrance of Blake's kiss came flooding back to her. She felt again the bruising intensity of his lips against hers, the strength of his powerful arms holding her close against him, and she suddenly realised that her frustration was as much physical as mental. Was that what was wrong with her? The very thought made her despise herself. A man took her in his arms and cold-bloodedly kissed her for no other reason than to teach her a lesson, and here she was mooning about the place like a lovesick schoolgirl! But it hadn't been cold-blooded; it had been warm and passionate. He had kissed her as though he meant it. Blake might despise her, might have set out to teach her a salutary lesson, but in that moment he had shown that he wasn't entirely immune to her.

And her feelings towards him? They were easy enough to define. She hated him as she had never hated anyone before in her life! Okay, so he had some good qualities, she would allow him that. His men respected and admired him: he was gentle and charming with the old and infirm, and the children flocked round him wherever he went, much as they followed Tansy. But against this he was a ruthless and dedicated soldier, and as such was Tansy's avowed enemy. There had been a declaration of war between them that afternoon and Tansy had no illusions about the conflict that lay ahead; she was up against a tough professional who would stop at nothing to achieve his own ends!

The golden light of the dawn filtered through the windows as Tansy rose from the chair where she had been dozing and stretched her aching muscles. John was sleeping peacefully, his pulse steady and even. She turned off the electric fan and tried to think when the next schooner was due as she needed more fuel for the generator. She wondered if her father would return on it. She sincerely hoped so; she felt a great need to have him near, to have the comfort and strength of his presence and advice. Going into the tiny bathroom, she washed her face and combed her hair, then went into John's room to fold the blanket she had used to cover herself and put it away in the store cupboard.

'Have you been here all night?'

Startled, Tansy turned to see Blake filling the doorway. 'Yes, John woke several times in the night and needed attention.'

'Couldn't your servant-girl have sat with him?'

'She could, but it's part of my job, not hers,' Tansy replied coolly.

'I'll send one of my men to take over while you get some sleep,' he said brusquely.

Tansy looked him over calmly and her voice was formal. 'That won't be necessary, Major Aston. Inara will give John his breakfast and I have a clinic to take this morning.'

'But it's Sunday,' he protested.

'That's why. Everyone comes to the church in the village on Sundays, some even from neighbouring islands, and they call in the clinic on the way. I get far more patients today than any other day. So, unless you want to see me about something . . .?' she finished pointedly.

'No, I came to see how John was progressing.'

'Why don't you go and see for yourself? He should be awake by now.'

He went in to John's room and stayed there for about

half an hour until Inara came, but Tansy didn't see him go; she was too busy preparing and making up medicines that she knew her regular patients would require when she saw them that morning.

When the church bell began to toll, doctor and patients tacitly called a halt and Tansy took off the overall she had put on over a simple white dress, and joined the throng of islanders making their way to the gothic church built of wood and grey lava-stone which stood among a grove of trees on slightly rising ground. The inside of the church was very beautiful. The walls were lined with coloured marble and stone carvings from the Hebrides, while the pews were of wood brought from the Solomon Islands, each pew end set in mother-of-pearl, patiently carved by island craftsmen, and adorned with rare shells.

As the people entered they each went to their allotted places, the women on the right, the men on the left, with the children in the front and the old people at the back. Tansy took her place with the girls of her own age group, many of them mothers several times over, quite often by different fathers. But on Aparoa it didn't matter; if you fell out of love there were no tears or jealous recriminations and you just went to live with someone else instead. If a baby came along and the parents didn't want to get married, then the grandparents or aunts and uncles would happily adopt the child and bring it up as their own. Tansy watched in some amusement as old Tupuhoe climbed into the pulpit. He always wore his best pinstriped suit on Sundays, one that Tansy had brought him back from England and of which he was inordinately proud. Ruari smiled at her from across the aisle and Tansy smiled easily back, but she looked at him with new eyes. Were his feelings for her more than those of a lifelong friend? She despised Blake for putting the thought in her mind, but it couldn't be so easily dismissed.

There was a noise in the doorway and the words, 'The officer,' were repeated on everyone's lips. Tansy turned and saw Blake standing in the aisle, head and shoulders above everyone else. He had two of his men with him and he quickly summed up the seating arrangements and led the men to a pew almost opposite her own. He looked across and caught her eye for a second, a sardonic smile playing on his lips. Flushing, Tansy turned away. This was carrying the war into the enemy's camp with a vengeance!

As there was no minister the service was entirely hymns and prayers, but Tansy found it impossible to concentrate; she was too aware of Blake's presence. Why had he come here? It certainly wasn't to impress the islanders with his piety! It was more likely to show his contempt of them, to impress them with his power to go anywhere and do anything he liked on Aparoa, she thought resentfully. The service over, they filed out, the eldest first. Blake had come out ahead of her and stopped to replace his beret on his dark hair that curled crisply into the nape of his neck. Deliberately Tansy walked past him as if he didn't exist and went up to Ruari, who immediately placed his arm across her shoulders as they walked down to the village together.

It was late in the afternoon before Tansy had dispensed the last bottle of medicine, listened sympathetically to the last list of symptoms and scolded the last patient for not taking more care of a festering wound. The natives tended to think that she had medicines to cure anything and as a result wouldn't look after themselves properly, so that wounds often became infected through neglect.

Rather wearily she went to see how John was and found him propped up reading one of the books on shells that she had lent him.

'How are you feeling?' she asked, and stuck a thermometer in his mouth before he could answer.

He mumbled something rather indignantly while Tansy took his pulse. 'My foot hurts like hell,' he complained when she removed the thermometer and marked up his chart.

'That's hardly surprising. Bulldozers are pretty heavy.' His temperature was up and his skin felt hot. 'I expect you'd like a bath?'

John looked at her, his face a picture of mixed emotions. 'Well, I ... er ...'

Tansy grinned. 'Don't worry. We have a male orderly for that kind of thing. I'll send him in to you.'

She went to arrange it and asked the orderly to stay with John while she and Inara went back to the house for a meal. Afterwards she sat on the veranda and looked across the bay. Some of the visitors from other islands were taking their white-sailed canoes through the coral reef to where the blue sea sparkled with light. They looked primitive and colourful, singing as they paddled, and Tansy wished that John could have seen them, for this was much more the South Pacific he imagined. She smiled to herself at his romantic idea of a tropical island, then sobered as she thought that the islanders had little enough reason for feasting at the moment. As she brooded on this, an idea began to form in her mind. By going to the church that day Blake had thrown the ball into her court and she rather thought that she saw a way to return it with a vengeance.

Forgetting everything else, she hurried down the road to Tupuhoe's house and found him and Ruari talking to a native girl, Lait. The two girls greeted each other warmly, for they were friendly, although Lait had a reputation—even among the Aparoans—for taking more lovers than anyone else. And there were plenty of men for her to choose from, for Lait was a beautiful young girl, her long wavy hair framing a round face with eyes as black as pools at night. She had a rich, full mouth and a splendidly proportioned body underneath her brightly coloured sarong, while in her hair she wore a wild orchid—on the left side to show that she was looking for a sweetheart. Ruari brought out some cans of beer which the four of them sat on the veranda to drink.

'Are there any feast days coming up soon?' Tansy asked casually.

Tupuhoe looked at her in some surprise. 'No, not unless someone decides to get married or have a birthday party.'

'Couldn't we invent a feast day? A really big one?'

'I suppose we could, but why?' the headman asked.

'A last fling before our life changes?' Ruari put in bitterly.

Slowly she replied, 'Well, no. I was thinking of using it as a cover.'

'As a cover? What for?'

Tansy looked at them steadily. 'A spot of sabotage.'

Ruari choked over his beer and Lait sympathetically slapped him on the back. 'Tansy, just what idea have you got in that mind of yours?'

'The soldiers have had everything their own way up to now. I think it's about time we started to retaliate,' she told him with a grin.

'How?' Ruari asked suspiciously.

'By stealing their explosives,' Tansy replied promptly.

They all stared at her and then Ruari let out his breath

in a low whistle, slowly shaking his head.

'It could work,' Tansy said quickly before he could object. 'If we told the soldiers that there was a big feast day and that it was the custom of the island that everyone should be invited, that it would be an insult to refuse, then they would have to attend and it would give us a clear field to steal the explosives—oh, and the detonators —we mustn't forget them. And you know something about engines, Ruari, you could sabotage the bulldozer. Put sugar in the petrol tank, perhaps.'

Ruari looked at her admiringly. 'You don't do things by halves, do you? It's a great idea, Tansy, but it wouldn't work. The Major is much too experienced to be caught by a trick like that. He'll insist on leaving at least one soldier to guard the explosives. And he'd keep a watchful eye open to see that nothing out of the ordinary was going on.'

'The guard we can deal with easily. We'll just take the feast to him. A few glasses of toddy or some even stronger drink and we'll be able to overpower him. They've stored the explosives in the cellar at the prison, and we know it isn't locked because old Amaru lost the key years ago.'

'And Major Aston?'

Tansy frowned. She had no illusions about deceiving Blake. He would be watchful as a cat, alert for signs of anything even slightly suspicious.

'I can look after the officer,' Lait broke in, and Tansy looked at her in surprise. 'I have seen him many times and he is one handsome man. Also he has looked on me and liked what he has seen,' she added complacently, running her hands down her hips. 'When I dance before him and give him food and drink from my own hands, then he will suspect nothing. And when I take him into the jungle it will be many hours before he starts again to think about his explosives.'

Tansy looked at her, knowing it was true. If Lait wanted a man, she got him. From the big grin on Ruari's face, Tansy strongly suspected that he, too, had fallen for her charms, and she felt a strong urge to slap the grin from his face. 'Well, I suppose that will work,' she said ungraciously. 'But we must see that all the soldiers are —er—entertained as well. Not having had any fresh food for so long they'll probably gorge themselves until they can't move anyway.'

'No, Tansy,' Ruari said firmly. 'Forget the whole thing. It's too risky. Somebody might get hurt and it's bound to land us in a lot of trouble.'

'But we've got to do *something*,' Tansy said desperately. 'We can't just sit back and let them take over the island.'

'Tansy is right,' Tupuhoe broke in unexpectedly. 'We are still men and we must fight for what is ours. We will carry out this plan.'

Ruari looked at their eager faces and then shrugged helplessly. 'All right, have it your way. After all, what have we got to lose?'

Tansy grinned at him. 'When shall we hold the feast?'

'It can't be done immediately,' Tupuhoe told her. 'We have to kill the animals and prepare the earth ovens in which to cook the food. Then the toddy and the other drink will have to be made and we will have to find a hiding-place for the explosives. It will take several days.'

'So long?' Tansy said in some dismay. 'But they might have started blasting and knocking the trees down by then. Still, I suppose it might lull them into a false sense of security.' Really, she thought, it was amazing how easily these military phrases came to her tongue!

They settled down to go into details of their plan and finally decided that Ruari should go to Blake that very day and invite the soldiers for the following Thursday.

'I will tell everyone in the village and have the oven dug,' Lait offered, her eyes bright with excitement and anticipation.

'Are you sure you don't want to ask the soldiers yourself, Tansy?' Tupuhoe asked.

'Good heavens, no! If I asked them they would be certain it was a trick.'

Ruari walked up with her to the house and went on up the road to the prison, while Tansy wondered just how Blake would receive the invitation. He would be extremely wary, she knew, and they would have to be very careful not to arouse his suspicions. But it would be interesting to see if the high and mighty Blake Aston would succumb to Lait's charms.

By Tuesday, John Andrews was well enough to be helped out of bed and to sit in a chair by the window, his foot perched on a stool. He was becoming extremely bored with being inactive, so Tansy had a couple of natives carry her father's chest of shells into his room and he happily set about arranging them properly.

'Are you sure your father won't mind?' he asked politely, his hands already hovering over the drawers.

'On the contrary, he'll be delighted. He always intended to do it, but just never seemed to get round to the job.'

'From what I've read, some of these are really superb specimens.' He glanced up at her. 'Blake tells me there's going to be a big feast day soon. Is it to commemorate something?'

'The anniversary of the election of the first chief,' Tansy invented rapidly.

'Am I going to miss it?' he asked wistfully.

'Certainly not! You're going to be carried out there in an armchair from the house and have a padded footstool for your leg. Everyone goes to this feast. Now, if you're comfortable, I have to leave you. The schooner is coming in and I have to make sure they've brought all the supplies I ordered.'

Already the jetty was crowded as the two-masted, white-painted schooner, its sails filled by the friendly trade winds, sailed towards the bay. Several canoes had gone out to meet it and everyone on the shore was filled with excitement as the boat was brought skilfully up against the stone jetty. Shouts of greeting filled the air, while the captain, a deeply tanned American, was hard pressed to keep the people from jumping on the deck before he had tied up. Tansy looked eagerly for her father and felt a sharp stab of disappointment when she saw that he wasn't on board.

Stores began to be unloaded while the native women crowded on the deck to buy lengths of brightly patterned cloth to make into new dresses for the feast, and their menfolk bartered for bottles of beer and rum. Several of the soldiers had come down to watch and soon some of them were buying souvenirs from the ship's stock; carved masks and items inlaid with beautifully worked mother-of-pearl. Tansy was checking her list of supplies when she noticed one of the soldiers further along the jetty examining a knife he had just bought. At that moment a drum of fuel-oil was being unloaded by a small crane and swung towards him. He jumped out of the way, but in doing so cut his thumb open with the sharp blade. He cursed loudly as the blood gushed out and dropped the knife, only to exclaim again as it fell into the sea. Without thinking the soldier kicked off his shoes and plunged down into the lagoon after it.

Tansy let fall her list and cried out a warning, but it was too late to stop him. She knew only too well that the open wound on his hand would attract the sharks within minutes once they caught the scent of blood. Tansy yelled to some mussel divers and they came running at her call, but before they could even get from the deck of the schooner to the jetty, a tall figure had come running forward, pulling a knife from his belt as he ran. Then Blake was diving cleanly into the water as a shark's fin broke the surface only fifty yards away. For a few moments the water was clear and Tansy could see Blake reach the other man and start to pull him towards the surface, then the shark came into view and Blake pushed the soldier behind him and turned to face it. The divers ran past her and plunged gracefully into the sea, almost as much at home in that element as on land, then the water frothed to a turmoil as all hell broke loose below the surface. The soldier who had gone in first was pulled out of the sea safely, but Tansy felt sick inside as a cloud of blood-soaked water swelled up from below.

Heads broke the surface then and Tansy felt a wave of dizzy relief as the other three men were quickly hauled on to the jetty. The water continued to boil as other black-finned sharks came quickly to the area and tore apart the dead shark that the men had killed. Pulling herself together, Tansy went over to see if any of them had been hurt. The soldier's thumb was badly gashed and would need a couple of stitches, but the natives were perfectly all right and had already gone unconcernedly back to their bartering. It wasn't until Blake turned round that she saw that the left side of his back was covered with blood beneath his torn shirt.

'It's nothing,' he said quickly when he realised that she had seen. 'It wasn't the shark, I scraped myself on some coral.'

'You'd better both come up to the clinic,' Tansy said rather breathlessly.

Once there, Blake motioned for her to treat the other man first and Tansy quickly did so, although she strongly suspected that Blake was hurt more than he admitted. The soldier was looking very shamefaced and took himself off hastily as soon as she had finished, obviously not liking the look in Blake's eyes that boded ill for him later.

'All right, Major, strip off and lie on the examination couch, please,' Tansy instructed as she went to wash her hands and prepare fresh dressings. She filled a hypodermic with antibiotic to prevent infection and turned with it in her hand. Blake was obediently lying on the couch all right, but he had taken off only his shirt and shorts.

'I thought I told you to strip,' she said tartly.

He turned slightly towards her and Tansy saw the mass of silky dark hairs on his broad chest. 'I know you did, but I'm not used to women doctors, especially young and attractive ones.'

Tansy realised that she had him at her mercy for the first time and she began to enjoy the situation. 'Oh, come now, Major, there's no need to be bashful. After all, as you said yourself, when you've seen one you've seen them all!'

His eyebrows flew up. 'Well, really, Doctor!' And he began to shake with laughter.

The full import of what she had said hit her and Tansy blushed to the roots of her hair. 'Oh! I didn't mean ...' With a quick, angry movement she pulled down the waistband of his pants and jabbed the needle viciously into his thigh.

'Ouch!' Despite the pain he continued to shake with silent laughter as Tansy cleaned up the gashes on his back, which luckily were merely superficial and would soon heal. She worked as quickly as she could and was none too gentle as she slapped on the antiseptic.

Turning away, she said coldly, 'You can get dressed now, Major. And there won't be any need for you to come again.'

'No, Doctor. Thank you, Doctor,' he said meekly as he put on his shorts and blood-stained shirt, but Tansy could still hear the laughter in his voice. Determinedly she kept her eyes on the instruments she was putting in the sterilizer, but was forced to turn round to look at him when he said, 'Oh, Doctor, there's just one thing.'

'Yes?' Tansy asked unwillingly.

'I'm sure you're extremely efficient, but your bedside manner leaves much to be desired!' Then he was gone, and the tin of antiseptic powder that Tansy threw at him cascaded only over the back of the door.

Indignantly she stared at the mess, her heart beating wildly and her fists clenched in rage. Then, absurdly, she began to giggle, slowly at first, but then really laughing with merriment. Damn the man! she thought as she wiped her eyes. How dare he make her laugh? Now it wasn't going to be so easy to hate him.

# CHAPTER SIX

THURSDAY dawned bright and clear and as Tansy pushed her window wide to look out across the bay she saw the red glow of sunrise lighten into the gold of early morning as the mists surrendered to the rising sun. Inara, too, was up and about and had her breakfast ready by the time Tansy returned from her morning shower under the waterfall. A sense of excitement pervaded the atmosphere as the two women made their way into the village to help with the preparations for the feast. There would be no clinic today—everyone was far too busy to feel ill. Children were running round carrying heavy pails of water from the spring, grating coconuts, or being generally put to use in a hundred ways. Perhaps it was because they were made to work so hard as little children that the islanders tended to become extremely lazy as they got older.

But today everyone was helping to make ready and was smiling and singing as they worked, although behind the sound of the people's voices Tansy could hear the raucous roar of the bulldozer's engine as it was used to clear the smaller plateau that ran at right angles to the coconut plantation. High in the blue sky a great hawk, sweeping overhead in long circles, had come down from the mountain and waited, ready to pounce on any small animal that ran from the danger of the encroaching bulldozer into open ground.

Three of the cattle had been slaughtered and their carcases had been roasting all night in the eight foot square by eighteen inches deep earth oven. This had been lined with stones on the bottom and a huge fire of palm logs built on them. When the stones became red hot, the ashes had been swept away and the food laid on the stones. Then big leaves were spread over the food and everything covered in sand. Now the women put in the chickens and joints of pork and started to prepare the vegetables and sauces. Great cauldrons were simmering over open fires ready to boil the piles of sweet potatoes and breadfruits, and the fishermen were out in the bay with nets and spears to catch the hundreds of fish that would be needed. More important still were the drums and pails of toddy and other native brews that were being collected together under a specially built shelter.

One cleaned-out oil-drum bubbled and frothed like a witch's cauldron, and Tansy asked the grinning native who watched over it what it contained.

'This is a special cocktail for the soldiers,' he told her. 'Three parts rum to two parts of coconut beer, and one part of those bottles of hair oil that we bought from the schooner last year and nobody wanted. We figured that would make it slip down real good.'

Tansy looked at him in horror as his grin widened even more. She hoped the soldiers would stick to the toddy or else there would be some bad hangovers the next day.

At noon the sound of the bulldozer stopped, and for a few minutes she could almost hear the blessed silence, so quickly had her ears become attuned to the continuous sound of the engine in the background. Before the feast there was to be a programme of native sports that would last the whole afternoon, and Tansy had promised John that he could come and watch these for an hour or so as long as he went back to the clinic to rest before the actual feast started. His leg was healing well and she would soon be able to remove the stitches; in which case, she thought with a trace of regret, she would have to relinquish her patient back to his comrades. She would be sorry to see him go, because she had enjoyed the many conversations they had had together when she kept him company during the day. After his first night at the clinic Blake had sent down his batman, who arrived punctually at ten every evening, to spend the night on a camp bed in John's room, thus relieving her of her vigil.

The batman was with John now and had helped him to dress in shirt and shorts against Tansy's orders, but his eyes were so full of eagerness at his reprieve from hospitalisation that Tansy didn't have the heart to do more than frown at him.

He grinned back at her like a small boy caught in some mischief. 'I refuse to go to my first feast in pyjamas and dressing gown. It would definitely be bad for my morale.'

'All right, you win this time. But remember, not more than a couple of hours this afternoon, and you're to promise to tell me at once if the heat gets too much for you. It's the first time you've been out for nearly a week and you must take things easily. If I think you're not up to it I won't let you go tonight,' she warned.

He agreed somewhat impatiently and Tansy supervised his transport to the open space in front of the meeting house in a chair carried by two of her stalwart rowers. A shade had been rigged up for him and Tansy carefully lifted his leg on to a footstool and made sure he was comfortable.

'I'm all right, really,' he assured her. 'Please, Tansy, don't fuss, I'm fine.' And he turned eagerly to watch a palm-climbing race between two young teenage boys.

'Your patient seems to be recovering,' Blake said drily,

overhearing John as he walked up to them. 'Especially if he's ill-mannered enough to abuse your care of him.'

John flushed and hastily apologised, which Tansy acknowledged with a slight nod before turning to walk away, but Blake caught up with her.

'Aren't you going to watch the sports?' he asked.

'Yes, but I wanted to get a flask of iced fruit juice from the fridge at the clinic in case John feels thirsty.' Tansy didn't look directly at him, she was afraid he might see the excitement in her eyes as she thought of what they were going to attempt that day.

'Then I'll walk with you, if I may?'

'That really isn't necessary, Major. I can manage perfectly well.'

'But I want to talk to you.' He put his hand under her elbow and drew her along the path to the clinic.

'Oh? What about?' Tansy tried to ask lightly. 'Is your back giving you trouble?'

'No, it's fine, thanks to you. All that antiseptic you put on seems to have done the trick.' There was an undertone of laughter in his voice that made her recall vividly their last meeting and her rough treatment of him. 'I wanted to ask you how John was coming along.'

'Very well. I was thinking earlier that I'd be able to take his stitches out soon, probably on Saturday to give him time to recover from today's festivities. You can arrange to collect him on Sunday, if that would suit you?'

'Good, I'm glad to hear it. I don't want to make your life a misery by leaving an impatient convalescent on your hands longer than necessary.' His manner was politely casual as Tansy walked along in the shade cast by his large frame.

'On the contrary, it's made a welcome change to have a European to talk to.'

He looked at her keenly. 'You miss your countrymen?'

'Not when Daddy's here, then we natter to each other all the time, but when he isn't I sometimes ...' She stopped, not wanting to give too much of herself away.

'Will he be back shortly?' The question was merely polite, not probing.

'I'm not sure. He's decided to have a holiday in Australia while he's there.' Then, not wanting him to think that her father had in any way deserted her, 'I don't suppose it will be for long. He usually can't wait to get back,' she said defiantly.

'Of course not,' Blake returned smoothly. 'Unless he's stopped running away.'

'Running away? What on earth do you mean?' Tansy stopped and looked at him in surprise.

Blake turned lazily to face her. 'All white men who settle in the tropics are running away from something.'

'That isn't true!' Tansy said indignantly, then added as she remembered some of the white men she had met in the Pacific, 'At least, not in my father's case.'

'Isn't it? Have you ever asked him why he came here?'

For a moment Tansy stared at him speechlessly, then turned abruptly and strode quickly towards the clinic, seething with anger at his temerity. Going into the clinic, she took a jug of iced lime-juice from the fridge and began to pour it into a vacuum flask. Some of the liquid spilled and spread a green stain over the white surface of the table. Blake came calmly over to her and took flask and jug from her shaking hands, doing the job deftly and efficiently.

'There,' he said, putting down the filled flask. 'Never try to do something like that until you've cooled down.'

'Why, you—you ...' Tansy's hands balled into tight fists as she struggled to keep her temper. 'How dare you make imputations about my father? You're not fit to even tread the ground he walks on, you're just a . . .'

'Really, Dr Harland, you mustn't let yourself get worked up so easily.' An amused smile lifted the corner of his mouth as he caught her wrists and held them at her sides. 'If you go on like this you'll be too upset to enjoy the feast tonight. And you do want to enjoy it, don't you? After all, a lot's going to happen tonight, isn't it?'

The question was slipped in so casually that, in her anger over his earlier remarks, Tansy almost missed it. She was on the point of blurting out exultantly that there certainly was, when she saw the pitfall opening before her and caught her breath to look into Blake's dark grey eyes watching her so closely. So that was it; he had suspected the invitation to be a trap and had deliberately baited her to make her so angry that she would give the plot away. She let out her breath on a long sigh and said icily, 'I don't have to stand here and listen to you. As far as I'm concerned I'd rather not attend the feast at all if you and your men are going to be there, but it happens to be a custom on the island that everyone should be invited—even the people who are wrecking it!' Snatching up the flask, Tansy hurried out of the clinic and this time he made no attempt to follow.

A hectic game of what Tansy always described as 'coconut football' between two villages was already under way when she returned to the clearing and dropped down on the grass beside John's chair. The 'pitch' was the length of ground as far as a man could run and the goalposts were coconut palms that, rather confusingly, could be attacked from both front and behind. There were nuts on the trees and occasionally one of these dropped heavily down on to one of the barefooted players, but the spectators thought this a good joke and hooted with laughter. Tupuhoe was the referee and stood on a high wooden box where he could see more easily. He had a whistle which he blew practically without stopping, though how he knew the rules Tansy could never discover, for they seemed to change every time she watched the game.

Blake strolled up and sat down on the grass on the other side of John, his face completely expressionless. Tansy would have given a lot to know what he was thinking, if he was still suspicious or whether she had managed not to give anything away, but she was kept busy with her first-aid treatment for the players; cuts, knocks and broken teeth were all taken in good part as the game progressed. At last the final whistle blew when the game was at a draw and all the players collapsed exhausted on the ground.

'That result hardly seems fair,' John exclaimed. 'Our village had the much better side. They deserved to win.'

'It doesn't matter which is the better side,' Tansy told him as she closed her bag and got to her feet. 'The match always ends in a draw because that's when Tupuhoe ends the game. If one side was allowed to win then all hell would let loose and the villagers would be fighting each other for weeks. This way we have the enjoyment of the game without any of the violence. You ought to try it in the U.K. some time,' she added, tongue in cheek. 'It would cure all that soccer hooliganism.'

Tansy saw John safely resting on his bed in the clinic before she, too, went home to rest before the night's activities. Inevitably her thoughts centred on their plans to steal the explosives and she dwelt with anticipation on Blake's reaction when he found them gone. That would pay him back for goading her this afternoon! She was

thankful that she hadn't fallen into the trap he had set for
her, but she would have to be careful—he might yet try
again. Restlessly, she turned on the bed, too full of excitement to be able to sleep. Tupuhoe had found a cave
on the side of the mountain in which to hide the dynamite, with another, smaller one for the detonators, keeping the two separate for safety's sake. The old chief had
entered into the plan with great zest and, despite Ruari's
misgivings, had organised everything down to the last
detail. Blake, of course, had been bound to be suspicious,
but had been able to get nothing out of the natives and
had probably only accepted the invitation because he
thought it might be a gesture of goodwill on the islanders'
part. Perhaps he hoped that the natives wanted to co-
operate with him after all, in defiance of her own wishes,
Tansy thought gleefully. Well, he was certainly going to
be in for a big surprise tomorrow morning!

She thumped her pillow aggressively, wishing it were
that smart-alec Major Aston, then caught sight of her
father's photograph on the bedside table. Thoughtfully
she reached out for it, a small frown between her brows,
then rolled on to her back to gaze up at the well-loved
features. He had taken the post on Aparoa over twenty
years ago, shortly after her mother's death, and had immediately flung all his time and energy into improving
the lot of the natives. During those years he had never
been back to England and had only twice been to
Australia for a short holiday, always hurrying back to
his beloved island. Even when Tansy and Ruari had
been at school in Sydney he had only escorted them there
on their first day and left them to make their own way
back to Aparoa for holidays. Teaching them to be independent, he had said, but now Tansy began to wonder.
Was it to help the natives that he had come to Aparoa?

Or was it to escape from a world he couldn't face without the wife he had loved so much?

Tansy stared at the photograph as so many things that had puzzled her over the years began to drop in place. His unwillingness even to have an assistant until Tansy had qualified: the leaves that he had never taken: the invitations from friends that he had always turned down until they ceased to come: how he had avoided as much as possible any other Europeans that came to the island. Only the impending threat of the fuel base had provoked him into going to Australia this time, and Tansy was amazed that he was staying there any longer than necessary. But perhaps he couldn't bear to see the island destroyed; he had put so much of himself into it over the years and now everything that he had done was to be ruined in a matter of days.

So that was another thing she had to thank Major Aston for, she thought bleakly. That her father didn't want to return to his own home! All right, perhaps at the beginning he had been running away, but he had found in Aparoa a place where he could live in contentment again, a place of sun and peace and laughter. He had fought to keep it that way and he had lost, so now it was up to Tansy to carry on as best she could. But she realised, as she drifted off to sleep at last, that not only Aparoa but she herself would never be the same again, for Blake had forced her to see the people she loved with different eyes. First Ruari and now her father. And she wished with all her heart that Blake Aston had never set foot on Aparoa.

It was evening when Tansy awoke, a beautiful starlit night heavy with the sense of anticipation that filled the atmosphere. She went to pick up her sarong, but, with her hand outstretched, she suddenly changed her mind and went instead to the wardrobe that contained her European clothing. Finger on lower lip, she deliberated for a few minutes and then drew out a dress of chiffon in muted shades of green that complemented her eyes. It had a full skirt caught in neatly at the waist, a gathered bodice and full bishop sleeves—a dress that covered her modestly but at the same time clung in all the right places. Her hair she put up in a soft yet sophisticated style and then applied a little make-up, green eye-shadow to match the dress and a pale coral lipstick. Critically she surveyed herself in the long dressing table mirror. There was something missing. Going to the window, she leant out and picked several of the white buds from the climbing rose that clung to the stonework. These she pinned carefully into place among the soft curls of her hair. Now she was ready. Like a warrior of old, she thought with a grin, she had donned her war-paint and was ready to go into battle.

John had slept well and was agog to set off. He had his camera with him and intended to compensate for his enforced inactivity by taking photographs of the celebrations. He whistled when he saw Tansy. 'I say, you look stunning. Whose benefit is it for?'

'Not for yours, anyway,' Tansy retorted. 'Look at the state of that bed! You're the worst patient I ever had.'

He grinned at her, quite unabashed, and Tansy saw him placed in his chair and carried off by the two natives while she stayed behind to strip and remake his bed. She heard a sound in the corridor and looked round to see Blake about to enter the room.

He stopped dead in the doorway at sight of her. 'Why, hello. I didn't expect to see you here.' He was breathing rather heavily as if he'd been hurrying.

'Did you want something, Major?' Tansy said into the

stillness that had suddenly filled the room.

'John forgot the flashgun for his camera.'

'It's over there, on the cabinet.' But he didn't attempt to get it. He merely leaned his shoulders against the door jamb and waited, as if prepared to settle there for the night.

Tansy turned her back on him while she finished the bed, then she straightened and moved purposefully towards the door. 'Please let me pass, Major Aston.'

His voice soft, he said, 'Don't run away. Let me look at you.' Then, 'You know, I was wrong.'

Finely arched brows raised, Tansy lifted her eyes to look into his. 'You? Wrong? I had thought that to be an impossibility,' she mocked him.

'Not in this case,' he answered with an appreciative gleam in his eyes. 'Because you're far more of a temptation now than you ever were in that sarong!' Then he had moved aside and she was free to pass.

Music was in the air as she neared the village. Someone put a flaming torch into her hand and drew her towards the cleared space where the islanders had formed two long lines facing inwards that stretched from in front of the meeting house almost to the edge of the jungle. Everyone held a lamp or flambeau of some sort and swayed to the rhythm of the drums energetically played by the musicians. There were European faces among the brown ones and Tansy wondered if Ruari had checked on how many soldiers were at the feast. Further along the line she saw John sitting in his chair, a swaying lamp in his hands, and the Major had been pulled into the line almost opposite. She smiled; the enemy was engaged—let battle commence!

Almost on the thought there came the sound of singing on the breeze and out from the jungle came twenty or so young men and girls, the men in pareus, the traditional native loincloths, with crowns of plaited pandanus leaves on their heads, and the girls in sarongs with garlands of white and yellow flowers round their necks and wrists and in their hair. They sang as they danced slowly and gracefully forward, triumphal songs and love songs that had been sung for hundreds of years—*Teki*, the natives called them. And among the dancers, looking lovelier than all the rest, was Lait, her undulating body swathed in a pale pink sarong that revealed the swell of her breasts.

When all the dancers had entered the clearing of coral sand, the two lines of spectators closed up to form a ring of light around them. The five men of the band with their drums made from hollowed-out branches of hard *Tou* wood, began to beat faster. Swaying and twisting to the pulsating music, the dances became livelier and wilder. The watching ring of onlookers clapped and sang, their torches bobbing to the rhythm. Faster and yet faster the dancers whirled as the drums throbbed their beat out into the night. Shadows leapt and danced among the palm trunks in the flickering, shifting light, as though they had been ghosts and spirits from a past age, wakened to life by the primitive, exciting music.

One by one the dancers dropped to the ground exhausted, until only Lait continued to spin and writhe to the now frenzied beat of the drums. Her long black hair one moment almost touched the ground as she leant backwards, the next was whirling round her head in a black cloud as she gyrated over the sand. Suddenly she raised her arms up high, spun madly for a few turns and then threw herself to the ground just as the drums ceased on a crescendo of sound, her outstretched arms pointing straight in Blake's direction. The long-drawn-out sighs from a hundred throats filled the sudden silence, but then the villagers smiled and nodded at Blake as he was urged forward to help Lait to her feet.

And he wasn't at all backward in doing so, either, Tansy noted wryly. Lait, being exhausted, had to cling to him as he solicitously helped her to sit down on one of the pandanus mats that had been spread ready for the feast. Somewhere in the background someone began to strum a guitar and the islanders laughingly took their places on the mats or went off to bring on the food. Tansy saw that John was already being taken care of by a smiling, dark-eyed girl who had been one of the dancers, so she walked casually round the edge of the circle to where Tupuhoe and Ruari sat just below the meeting house. She smiled exultantly when she reached them; all but two of the soldiers were at the feast, one of the absentees being the man who had attacked her.

The two men smiled back at her, guessing her thoughts, and Tupuhoe politely cut off a large piece of the whole pig that was in front of him and passed it to her, his eyes twinkling with merriment.

'You look very European tonight,' Ruari remarked as he helped himself to roast karava fish and breadfruit. 'Why aren't you wearing your sarong like the other women?'

'Perhaps because I am a European,' Tansy replied gently.

Ruari stopped what he was doing and turned to look into her eyes. 'Ah, yes, I tend to forget that.'

'I know. So do I.' Then Tansy smiled at him. 'But I'm glad you do.'

He smiled back, rather wryly, but Tansy turned as she felt someone watching her. But whoever it was must have looked quickly away, for she had no one's attention now. John was busily taking photos from his chair and Blake and the other soldiers were intent on the food in front of them and the native girls at their sides, although Tansy noticed that most of them held coconut cups of the special 'cocktail' in their hands.

Older men and women gradually began to get to their feet whenever they felt like it and would perform ancient dances or would sing. Half a dozen men chanted an old, old war song, performing the actions of paddling the long since gone war canoes and waving spear and knife, while others murmured in unison in the background and the drums beat softly, hardly louder than the white breakers that washed upon the nearby shore. Tansy felt a gentle touch on her arm and knew that Ruari was slipping away to the prison. Already the guards had been taken food and plenty of drink by two village girls, and they hoped that by the time Ruari and the young men he had chosen to help him got there, the guards would hardly be in a state to offer any resistance.

The drums began to beat faster again as the war dance reached its climax and Tansy felt her heart beating as fast as the music. Would they be successful? Would they? Others got up to dance, some of the girls pulling the soldiers up to join in. They were embarrassed at first, moving sheepishly, but as the beat got to them they soon lost their inhibitions and kept time with the throbbing music. A space cleared momentarily and Tansy was able to look across the circle to find Blake staring at her, the flickering light giving him a fierce, devilish look. For a moment their glances locked, then the dancers closed together again and when Tansy next saw him he had his arm round Lait and was taking the flower from her hair to put in his buttonhole.

It seemed a very long time, but in fact was less than

an hour, before Ruari slipped quietly back into his place beside her, and there was no need for Tansy to ask the eager questions that trembled on her lips—the triumphant look in his eyes told her all she wanted to know!

There were one or two gaps on the mats now as the heady music and wine led the younger people to steal off in couples into the scented privacy of the jungle, some of the soldiers among them. Another young private collapsed in a heap and Tansy saw Blake get to his feet and walk over to him. Apparently satisfied that he was only sleeping, he straightened up as Lait came to stand close beside him. She smiled at him enticingly and took the flower from his buttonhole to place it in the top of her sarong, in the deep V formed by the curve of her breasts. Blake smiled lazily down at her and allowed Lait to lead him into the darkness of the jungle.

Tansy stood up abruptly. 'I have to see to my patient.'

Ruari looked at her in some astonishment. 'Don't you want to hear how we got on?'

'Oh! Oh, yes, of course.' For the moment Tansy had forgotten the purpose of this entire exercise.

Almost reluctantly she sat down again and listened with only half an ear as Ruari described his exploits. 'The two sentries weren't even on guard,' he told her jubilantly. 'The girls had persuaded them to go down to the river to swim, so we were able to sneak in and down to the cellars. There were ten boxes of explosives; we broke them open and packed the dynamite into old beer kegs and then replaced the boxes so that the locks didn't show. Then we did the same with the detonators. With any luck no one will notice they're empty until they go to use them,' he chuckled. 'After we'd got the explosives we crept out without being seen and I left the other men to load up your pony cart. They should be on their way to the mountain now, but I thought I'd better come back in case the Major noticed I was missing.' He waited for Tansy to say something, but when she didn't he added impatiently, 'Well, what do you think? Aren't you pleased with what we've done?'

'Yes, more than pleased. It's all worked out beauti- fully, far better than I'd dared to hope. But what about the bulldozer? Weren't you able to do anything to that?'

For answer, Ruari grinned broadly and opened his hand to show her an oily piece of complicatedly shaped metal with holes either end. To Tansy it looked just like a piece of scrap, but Ruari assured her that the bulldozer couldn't possibly go without it.

Tupuhoe leaned across and took it from Ruari's hands. 'If the machine is useless without this then it must be worth much money. I will thread it on some twine and wear it as a necklace.' Then he laughed deep in his throat and Ruari and Tansy joined in his merriment.

But, although Tansy joined in the laughter and exult- ant murmurs that rose from the other islanders as they learnt the good news, she couldn't help staring across at the heavily scented jungle. It would serve Blake right, she thought malevolently. He was an arrogant, imposs- ible man whom she loathed, and she couldn't care less if he was demoted, or whatever happened as a punishment in the army. So why did she have this terribly empty kind of feeling whenever she thought of the way he had smiled down at Lait through heavy-lidded eyes, and the way he had put his arm so familiarly round the girl's waist as they had entered the jungle? She hadn't really expected anything else of him, had she? He was just a boorish soldier, no different from the others. He had proved that by the way he had kissed her on the beach. But there was a lost, wistful look in Tansy's eyes as she again remembered that kiss, a kiss that had left her with the distinct impression that he had meant every breathtaking second of it.

One of her native rowers was trying to catch her attention and she looked at him rather dazedly. 'Yes, Teiho, what is it?'

'The young officer. He's ready to go back now.'

Hastily Tansy hurried over to where John lolled in his chair, half asleep. Guiltily she felt his pulse, but he opened his eyes and smiled at her. 'I think the party's over, don't you?'

Tansy laughingly agreed with him, walking along beside his chair and waiting until the natives had helped him to undress and get into bed before making her own way slowly back to the house. Of Inara there was no sign, and Tansy was pretty certain that she would see nothing more of her intended chaperone that night. The pony was back in his stable and Tansy checked to see that the trap showed no signs of the illicit use to which it had been put before going to her room. Crossing to the window, she looked out across the bay, but somehow the beauty of the night failed to give her the peace and tranquillity which usually entered her heart whenever she saw it. Instead she was filled with desolation, her mind tormented by a wretchedness worse than she had ever known.

# CHAPTER SEVEN

SLOWLY Tansy came to wakefulness the next morning to the dim realisation that there must be a heavy thunderstorm outside, for she could hear loud noises in the distance. Her head felt thick and heavy as she rather dazedly opened her eyes and saw that it was bright daylight. It had been almost dawn before she had at last got to sleep, and she moaned when she saw that it was still only seven o'clock. Gradually it penetrated her mind that if the sun was shining there couldn't be a thunderstorm, that the bangs she could hear must be someone knocking at the door. Pulling on a turquoise bathrobe over her short nightie, her hair gloriously tousled, she groped her way downstairs, her head aching abominably from her sleepless night and the toddy she had drunk at the feast.

'All right, all right, I'm coming!' she called as she struggled to pull open the heavy old oak door.

The last few inches came open with a rush as a burly arm pushed it back. Tansy found herself staring at Blake, but she had only time to note the ferocious look on his face before he had swept her back into the living room.

'All right, where is it?' he demanded with scarcely controlled rage.

'Oh, it's you.' Tansy wandered over to the settee and curled up on the cushions, too tired to be intimidated. 'You wouldn't like to make me some coffee, would you? I have a headache.'

114

'No, I would *not* like to make you coffee,' he almost snarled. 'Now where is it?' He had come to stand menacingly over her, holding his swagger-stick in white-knuckled fists, very much as if he would have liked to use it.

'You know something?' Tansy said as she leant her head back to look up at him towering over her. 'You really should learn to control yourself more, Major. You're supposed to be in charge of all those men and yet you ...' She broke off abruptly as Blake caught hold of her arms, pulled her round into a sitting position, and shook her vigorously until her teeth rattled.

'Wake up, Tansy. Wake up!'

He let her go and Tansy stared at him, now fully awake as she realised belatedly why he had come. So he had missed the dynamite already. She wondered if he had been out all night and had just got back to the prison, but his shirt and shorts were clean and pressed and he looked fresh and rested. Which was more than what she felt, she thought resentfully. Irritably she got to her feet and pushed him aside.

'Where do you think you're going?' He caught her arm again.

'To the bathroom,' Tansy said with some dignity. 'I told you, I have a headache and I want to take an aspirin.'

Blake looked at her for a minute, his eyes narrowed, then let her go. 'All right, but hurry up—and don't try anything.'

Tansy glared at him and deliberately took her time as she dressed, brushing her hair back from her head and fastening it in place at her nape with a clip. When she came down again Blake called out from the kitchen and she went reluctantly to join him. He had made two steaming mugs of coffee and pushed one towards her before sitting down at the pine table.

'You make very free of my home, Major,' she said sarcastically.

'You asked me to make it, remember?' He looked at her clean, unmade-up face and remarked, 'You look about sixteen years old.'

Tansy's eyelids flew up and then were quickly lowered as she concentrated on the hot, reviving coffee.

'And you act like a sixteen-year-old,' he added caustically. 'I bet it was your idea to sabotage the bulldozer. Well, I want the part back, Tansy, and I mean to get it, make no mistake about that.'

Quickly Tansy looked away, afraid that he might see the gleam in her eyes as she realised that he hadn't yet discovered the loss of the explosives. Well, he wouldn't find the part here, and she was going to enjoy revelling in his discomfiture. 'I don't remember ever giving you permission to use my christian name,' she said coldly.

'I don't need permission. I can do anything I want on this island—that goes for you as well as the natives. Do you want me to send my men to search this house and every other house in the village? I can, you know. My orders give me carte blanche over Aparoa—and its inhabitants.'

Tansy looked at him scornfully. 'Really, Major, all this fuss over a missing engine part! One of your men probably lost it and was too scared to own up. I bet they're all afraid of you and your vicious temper,' she goaded.

His lips tightened for a moment. 'How did you know it was a part of the engine? I didn't say it was.'

'What? Well, it would have to be a part of the engine, wouldn't it? Otherwise I would have heard it. The darn thing makes so much noise that the whole of Aparoa can hear it,' she countered.

Rising to his feet, Blake picked up his beret and put it on.

'What, leaving so soon, Major? But you haven't finished your coffee,' she said with spurious regret.

'Wherever the part is, it isn't here—you're too damn sure of yourself for that. I shall just have to try elsewhere, won't I? Perhaps I'll try your boy-friend next,' he suggested, watching her closely.

But Tansy had expected that one and ignored it completely. 'Did you enjoy the feast, Major?' she asked sweetly. 'You seemed to be having quite a good time. I hope that Lait—er—looked after you satisfactorily?'

He had walked towards the door and opened it before he turned back to answer her. 'Yes, thank you, Dr Harland. She looked after me very well—in fact I can't think of a time when I've been more—completely satisfied!' And then he was gone.

Going down to the clinic later, Tansy tried not to think of what Blake might be doing in the village. She heard the sound of the jeep's engine and wished she had thought of getting Ruari to sabotage that too. Would Tupuhoe have hidden the part in a safe place? It was most unlikely that Blake would ever find it short of tearing Tupuhoe's house apart, and even then the headman might have hidden it outside the house. Her spirits revived as the morning wore on and her patients brought her the latest news; Blake had put a guard outside Tupuhoe's house and prevented anyone from going in; ten of the soldiers were searching the island for Ruari, another two had taken over the blacksmith's lean-to and were trying to forge a new part. Tansy smiled to herself; Tupuhoe had probably switched off his hearing-aid and Ruari had departed the island by canoe at first light—as the only one who knew anything about engines he was the obvious suspect and better out of the way. And as for the engine part—Tansy chuckled as she remembered its intricacies—it would take them days to get it right, if they managed it at all.

It was nearly noon before the last patient had gone and Tansy was beginning to long for lunch and a rest before going on her rounds. She slipped off her white coat at last and hurried out of the clinic. Blake was leaning against a tree trunk a few yards away, his arms folded, patiently waiting for her as if nothing was wrong, as if his whole career wasn't in jeopardy.

'Why, Major Aston, what a surprise! Have you solved the mystery of the disappearing engine part?' she taunted him.

'Not yet, but I expect to at any moment,' he replied equably, falling into step beside her. 'Where's your boy-friend?'

'My boy-friend, as you insist on calling him, has gone to visit relatives.'

'Oh, where?'

'I'm afraid I really couldn't say; he has relatives all over Aparoa,' Tansy replied airily.

'Which means that he's done a bunk and probably isn't on the island at all,' Blake responded dryly. 'In that case I have no choice.'

'No choice about what?' Tansy asked guardedly.

'You'll see. Get in the jeep, please.' His manner changed suddenly and he became curt and authoritative.

'Why? What for?'

But he didn't bother to answer, just propelled her to the waiting jeep where two soldiers stood guarding it, and Tansy saw with a sick feeling that they both carried rifles.

'Get in, Dr Harland.'

Tansy looked round at Blake uncertainly, but his eyes were cold as steel. Her heart sinking, she reluctantly obeyed him.

'Where are you taking me?' she demanded as he climbed in beside her and the jeep moved off.

He didn't even bother to look at her as he said matter-of-factly, 'To the prison. I'm putting you under arrest.'

Gazing at him in utter stupefaction, Tansy gasped, 'But—but you can't do that!'

Then he looked at her in derisive amusement. 'I told you, I can do anything I consider necessary.'

A cold chill of fear began to touch her, but she said bravely, 'You're bluffing to try to frighten me. Anyway, you can't use those cells in the prison any more, none of the locks have got keys.'

'They have now,' he replied calmly, his face expressionless. 'That's what my men were making at the forge this morning. I let it be known they were trying to make a replacement part in case you got the wind up and tried to get away. They finished the keys some time ago, but I thought I'd let you finish your clinic before I arrested you.'

'That's very big of you,' Tansy said sarcastically, then twisted round to look at the passing scenery, unwilling to let him see the consternation on her face. She had never thought that he would go this far; he must be bluffing, he must be! But when they drove through the gallows gate where convicts had once been hanged for all to see, and drew up in the courtyard, he merely said,

'Put her in the cell, Sergeant,' turned on his heel and marched away.

For a moment Tansy stared after him, at his ramrod-straight back and the arrogant thrust of his chin, but then the sergeant said, 'This way, miss,' and led her down a dark stairway, along an echoing passageway and then down some more stairs. Tansy knew where they were going, she had often played here as a child. She knew that down here were the dank cells without light and fresh air where the toughest prisoners had been manacled to the walls for weeks and months on end, without hope, without the mercy of death.

Despite all her attempts at fortitude, she drew back with a shudder as the sergeant pulled upon the massive iron door with a trap for the jailor to look through, and motioned her to go inside. She looked at him pleadingly.

'Sorry, miss. Major's orders.'

Then Tansy's chin came up. She wouldn't let him think she was afraid. So with her head high she stepped boldly into the cell. The heavy door clanged shut behind her, she heard the key turn in the lock, then the trap in the door was closed and she was left in total darkness!

Carefully she groped her way to the opposite wall and leaned against it, only to stand up quickly again as the cold, damp stones touched her skin. The cell must be under the stream that served the prison with drinking water and had seeped down through the old walls. In the light from the corridor when she had entered she had seen that the cell was completely bare, no bed or chair, nothing! If Blake had it in mind to wear her down then he was going all out to do it. No holds barred. She wouldn't give in, she thought defiantly. She could take the cold, the damp, and the darkness, take that and more besides before she would let him win this battle.

When next someone came to the cell and opened the trap Tansy was standing in the far corner, huddled against the wall with her arms wrapped round herself to try to keep warm. She gazed at the small square of light as a person lost in the desert gazes at a mirage. Then the light was blocked out as someone looked in on her. She heard an explosive bellow of rage and recognised Tupuhoe's voice. So that was Blake's ploy; to hold her as a hostage until Tupuhoe gave up the engine part. Fiercely she hoped that he wouldn't give in. But Tupuhoe looked upon her as a daughter and would be terribly angry and upset at seeing her in these conditions, which was precisely why Blake had let him see her.

Running to the door, Tansy tried to call out to him that she was all right, not to give in. But the sergeant immediately slammed the metal trap shut and the darkness closed in again.

For a long time her thoughts raced as she wondered what was happening in the prison office above her, then the outside images faded and she became aware only of her surroundings. The cold became more intense and she began to shiver uncontrollably. Her legs ached with standing and she longed to sit down, but the floor was wet with slime from the drops of moisture that fell from the ceiling, often dripping on her in the darkness and frightening her until she realised what they were. As the time dragged on she became hungry and thirsty, not having eaten since the early morning, and then only coffee and toast. The silence was intense, only the plop of the drips of water convincing her that she hadn't gone deaf. Then she heard a slight sound in the corner. At first she thought she was mistaken, but then it came again— a small, scratching sound. Tansy felt her skin begin to prickle with fear as well as with cold. She tried to back away, but was brought up short by the wall, her breath coming in little sobbing pants of fear. The noise came again, nearer, and little beads of perspiration broke out on her forehead as she stared wild-eyed into the impenetrable darkness.

Then something wet and furry brushed against her

bare ankles. Tansy screamed in agonised terror and threw herself across the cell, groping frantically for the door. Frenziedly she beat against the iron panels with her fists, her screams filling the cell. By the time the sergeant got the door open she was on her knees in front of it, sobbing hysterically as she continued to beat upon it. The man lifted her to her feet and half dragged, half carried her up flights of stairs and along a corridor as she held on to him desperately, unable to feel anything but that moment of panic-stricken terror.

He pushed open a door and led her into a room where the sunlight was so bright that it hurt her eyes and she put her hands up to shield them. There were confused noises around her, of surprise, of anger. Someone sat her in a chair and gave her something to drink, but her hands were shaking so much that she couldn't hold the glass so somebody held it for her. It must have been brandy or some other spirit, because it made her choke and she tried to push it away. But whoever was holding it said, 'Drink it!' in a harsh, commanding voice. When she obeyed it brought warmth and feeling flooding back, although her teeth still chattered from cold and fright.

A warm blanket was put round her shoulders and somebody began to rub her hands vigorously. Opening her eyes properly at last, she saw that it was Tupuhoe, his lined face filled with concern. The next instant she was held fast in his arms as he muttered curses a thousand years old at someone behind her. Slowly Tansy raised her head and saw that she was in the converted office in the prison and that there were several people in the room. Besides Tupuhoe, dressed in his best Sunday suit, there was the sergeant, and two other soldiers who stood on either side of the door, and standing near the window, holding the glass from which she had just drunk and gazing back at her, was Blake Aston. His lips were drawn into a grim line in his set face and there was a look in his eyes of intense inner anger, held firmly in check.

Tansy turned away from him, aware of her hair clinging damply to her head, of the smears of dirt and green slime on her clothes. Looking up at Tupuhoe, she managed a smile and said in a voice that belied her words, 'I'm fine now. Really I am.'

Blake's voice behind her said, 'In that case you can be returned to your cell.'

Blake couldn't see the way that her face blanched with fear, but Tupuhoe could. Holding her hands tightly, he turned to Blake and said indignantly in English, 'You cannot do this to her. It is cruel.'

'The remedy is in your hands,' Blake replied coldly. 'Return the part you took from the bulldozer and Dr Harland is free to go.'

Tansy stood up, trying not to tremble, not to think ahead. 'I'm quite ready to go back.' Then quietly to Tupuhoe in Polynesian, 'I'm all right. It was only a rat that scared me. I won't be afraid any more. Please don't let him win.'

The headman sadly shook his grey head. 'You are very brave, my daughter, but I cannot let you do this.' He looked over her head at Blake. 'You will give me your word that you will let Tansy go?'

'You already have it.'

Loosening his tie, Tupuhoe undid the top button of his shirt, revealing the part on a string round his neck. It had been carefully cleaned and polished until it shone. He placed it on the long table and Tansy heard Blake step briskly over to pick it up and examine it.

'It's still in good order. Very well, Dr Harland, you

can go. The sergeant will escort you home.'

'I will take Tansy home,' Tupuhoe intervened.

'I'm afraid that won't be possible. You are still under arrest, Tupuhoe,' Blake said crisply.

Then Tansy turned to stare at him. 'Why?' she burst out. 'As a guarantee of our future good behaviour? You've got your damn bulldozer back in one piece. What more do you want?'

'There is still the matter of the missing explosives,' he replied evenly.

Tansy felt as if her legs had suddenly gone limp. 'When did you find out?' she asked dully.

'As soon as I returned here after the feast. The thieves had neglected to cover the tracks of the horse and cart. There hadn't been any horses near the prison since you forbade everyone to sell us food, so it was easy enough to follow the tracks as far as your stable. I soon found the dynamite was missing and then checked on the bull-dozer.'

'But why did you only ask about the engine part?' Tansy said in bewilderment. 'Surely the dynamite was much more important?'

'I really don't think it necessary to explain my methods to you, Dr Harland,' Blake said coldly. He looked at the sergeant and nodded towards Tupuhoe. 'Take the old man and put him in the same cell the woman was in.'

Then Tansy saw it all. He had played on Tupuhoe's feelings for her to get the bulldozer part back and now he was going to use her feelings for Tupuhoe to get the explosives. Her face bleak, she crossed the room to stand opposite him. 'You can't do that, and you know it. Tupu-hoe is an old man and he suffers from asthma.' She could have added that too many hours in the damp cell could kill him, but she didn't have to; Blake knew that already.

'I shall do what I have to, Dr Harland. That dynamite could be dangerous if it got into the wrong hands. Do you want someone to get blown to pieces because of your folly?'

'Oh, it's very well hidden, where no one, especially you, will ever find it,' Tansy retorted.

Scathingly he said, 'There's really no point in holding out. I can always have more dynamite brought to the island.'

'But not without making yourself look a fool in the eyes of your superior officers! And that's what this is all about, isn't it?' Tansy said, her face set in lines of utter contempt. 'You have to get the explosives back because you just can't bear to think that a tribe of primitive natives got the better of you! That's why you're threatening a woman and an old man. You're a coward, Major! A despicable coward!'

Blake's eyes stared into hers, the pulse at his temple beating fast as his face darkened. With a loud crack a pencil he had been holding snapped in two. He took a deep breath before he said, 'Do I put him in the cell or don't I?'

Tansy suddenly felt very tired. 'No. I'll tell you where it is.' She went slowly to the open window and leant against the stone surround, feeling completely drained of energy. They had had such high hopes of their plot, but Blake had beaten them hollow, got back everything that was lost in less than a day. In the room behind her she could hear orders being given, the door opening and closing, marching feet on stone, then she saw Tupuhoe being escorted across the courtyard to walk freely through the gateway.

Raising her eyes, she saw that the sun had already begun its descent and realised that she must have been locked in the cell for over two hours, then hastily thrust the memory of that terrible time away from her thoughts. Except for the mountain, this was one of the highest points on the island and she could just make out the tips of the palm trees on one of the tiny coral atolls far out on the horizon, turned now to gold in the shafts of the sun. Her eyes gradually widened as an idea occurred to her. Suppose she told Blake that the explosives were hidden somewhere else? The idea, once born, began rapidly to be enlarged and she had to put on a careful act of deep dejection when she turned round, in case anyone saw the light of hope deep in her eyes.

But there was only Blake in the room, leaning against the table, quietly waiting for her. He straightened up as she turned and said, 'Would you like another drink?'

Tansy shook her head wordlessly.

'I expect you'd like to change before we go.'

'Go?'

'I think it would be best if you showed me yourself exactly where the explosives are hidden.'

Tansy raised her eyes to his for a moment and then lowered them. 'Of course, you would want that, wouldn't you?'

He held the door open for her and she walked ahead of him out of the prison. Out in the road she stumbled over a stone and Blake went to help her, but Tansy wrenched her arm away and glared at him with deep hatred in her eyes. 'Don't you dare touch me!'

He opened his mouth to say something, then shut it in a grim line and stepped back to let her precede him into the jeep. At the house he followed her inside. Inara came from the kitchen and exclaimed with horror when she saw the state that Tansy was in. The normally placid native woman poured a stream of murderous Polynesian at Blake's head until Tansy broke in to ask her to make her something to eat. The cool, clean water of the shower was a delight as Tansy scrubbed herself clean of the filth from the cell, using her favourite scented soap to take away the smell of that dank place. Towel-drying her hair, she put on clean slacks and a sweater, knowing that she might need it before the day was out.

Blake was waiting in the hallway, but Tansy ignored him and went into the kitchen to eat the omelette Inara had prepared for her. Not until she had finished did she look at him. 'What have you done with Tupuhoe?' she asked.

He stirred in the chair where he had been waiting in apparent patience. 'He's under house arrest. The guard will be removed as soon as I have the explosives back safely. Where on the island is it hidden? Can we get there by jeep?'

Tansy schooled her features into a disdainful look. 'You don't think we'd be foolish enough to hide it on Aparoa, do you? It's on another island entirely.'

She turned to despondently take an orange from the overloaded fruit bowl on the table, her heart beating against her ribs. That Blake didn't trust her an inch she was quite certain, but her listless manner must have convinced him, because he said, 'I'll order my men to have the boat made ready for sea.'

'That won't be necessary. Your beautiful boat would be useless. It's hidden on a coral atoll that can only be reached by canoe. I'll order my rowers to have my canoe made ready,' she added in sarcastic imitation of his tone.

'So you're coming back to life, are you? If you're

ready we'd better leave at once,' he added pointedly.

Tansy rose with feigned reluctance and let him drive her down to the harbour. Once there she turned to ask one of the children to fetch Teiho and the others, but Blake stopped her.

'Oh, no, you don't. I don't intend to be outnumbered on this trip. You and I are going alone.'

'But—but it's a long way,' said Tansy, trying to hide her consternation.

'Then we'd better get going, hadn't we?'

Before she had time to protest or think of some way of making him change his mind, Tansy found herself in the prow of a canoe with Blake kneeling in the stern, propelling it strongly through the water.

'I didn't know you could paddle a canoe,' Tansy remarked waspishly.

'So now you do. Turn round and look out for coral-heads.'

Rather sulkily Tansy obeyed him, knowing that their safety would depend on her watchfulness. Once outside the harbour, Blake put up the sail that sent the canoe gliding through water so clear that she could see rocks and shells, and fish swimming in the translucent green depths below as the waves of the great ocean formed and fled in the golden sunlight. It was a silent journey except when she told him in which direction to steer, for she was busily thinking ahead to how she would handle the situation when they reached the coral atoll.

At length the tops of its few trees and shrubs came into view and Tansy leant back to pick up another paddle. 'We have to go round to the other side of the island.'

Carefully they paddled round, holding the canoe back from the tide that threatened to carry it on to the reef. On the lee side of the island an outcrop of rocks jutted out to sea and Tansy steered towards them. 'It will be better if you jump for the rocks,' she called back over her shoulder without taking her eyes from the dangerous shore. 'Then you can catch hold of the canoe while I get out and we can lift it over the rocks into the lagoon.'

'Isn't there a way through the reef?' Blake almost had to shout above the roar of the surf.

'Yes, but it's very small. My rowers know it, but I'm not sure. It will be safer the other way. Or else we can go back and get the natives,' she added to press home her point.

He hesitated, then, 'No, we'll do as you say. Take her in close and try and hold her steady.'

A quick look over her shoulder showed her Blake braced to jump as she took advantage of a wave to go in near to a big, flat-topped rock. She felt the canoe lighten with a jerk as he leapt out. One look ensured that he had landed safely and was picking himself up, and then she had the paddle dipping deeply into the water and scudding dangerously near the reef as she put as much distance as she could between them. She heard a shout behind her, but took no notice. Let the hateful man find out for himself what it was like to be alone and cold in the dark, but on a deserted island instead of in a damp cell!

The canoe surged joyously through the water as she put all her strength and skill into sending it flying through the waves. When she had covered a fair distance she glanced back for a last triumphant look at Blake stranded in his rock prison—but he was no longer there! Instead she saw his dark head cutting through the water not thirty yards behind her. Panic-stricken, she dipped the paddle in the sea again, but fumbled and almost dropped it. The fool! He couldn't possibly hope to catch her, especially swimming against the tide. But he was still coming on relentlessly. Then Tansy froze with the paddle in mid-stroke as she remembered the grazes on his back that hadn't yet healed. If a shark got the scent of them!

He was much closer now and she turned the canoe broadside on to let him catch up and climb aboard. Again he had outsmarted her, and she knew that she would have to give up her plan to abandon him on the atoll and take him back to Aparoa, there to face the consequences of her actions. Blake was only a few yards away and still swimming strongly when Tansy thought she saw a movement in the water just behind him. Quickly she stood up and lifted the heavy paddle in both hands, raising it high above her head to try to beat off any attack until Blake got into the boat.

Lifting his head from the water, he saw her above him and raised an arm to catch hold of the side of the canoe, but instead of hoisting himself into it as she expected, he suddenly brought all his pressure to bear and turned the canoe over, pitching her headfirst into the sea. Her first thought was that a shark must have got him and she beat the water and shouted as loudly as she could in the hope of driving it away. But then she found herself caught in a powerful grip as Blake took hold of her. She tried to struggle free to reach the upturned canoe, but he only held her tighter, catching her under the arms and turning on his back to swim her along with him back towards the atoll. The sound of the surf breaking over the reef became even louder now and she forgot all about the shark as the tide carried them inexorably nearer.

A long, curling breaker picked them up as easily as a scrap of driftwood and surged forward towards the reef. The roaring noise of the sea filled her ears and she found that she had turned in Blake's arms and was clinging to him as tightly as he was holding her. She felt sharp points catching at her clothes and then the wave had carried them over the reef into the calm waters of a small lagoon.

The force of the wave had left her limp and exhausted so that she had to lie gasping on the sand when Blake at last pulled her out of the sea. He, too, collapsed on the beach, his chest heaving as he tried to recover his breath.

'You—all right?' His voice rasped in his throat.

'Y-yes. You?'

He didn't answer, but Tansy saw him nod as he raised himself on one elbow. They lay there until their breathing steadied, then Blake stood up and began to walk along the waterline. Tansy sat up, alarm in her eyes.

'Where are you going?'

Blake looked at her briefly. 'To see if there's any sign of the canoe.'

He walked off, his feet leaving footprints in the virgin-white sand, and Tansy tried to wring some of the water from her clothes; her shoes she had lost in the sea. Five minutes later he returned without seeing any sign of the canoe.

'It probably broke up on the reef,' Tansy remarked. 'We were lucky not to get caught on it ourselves. It was a pity about the canoe. I thought the shark had got you when you overturned it.' She ran her fingers through her hair, trying to untangle it.

'Shark? What shark?' Blake crouched down beside her as Tansy turned to stare at him.

'I thought I saw a shark behind you. Why else did you overturn the boat instead of climbing into it?'

There was a disbelieving curl to his lip as Blake retorted, 'Because I didn't want to have my head smashed in by the paddle! I knew you hated me, lady, but by God, I didn't think you'd go that far!'

Tansy stared back at him, shocked horror in her eyes. 'You thought I was going to hit you?' She spoke almost in a whisper. The enormity of the accusation held her stunned for a moment, then she scrambled hastily to her feet and glowered down at him resentfully. 'I wish the sharks had got you! I wish you'd drowned in the sea! But most of all I wish you'd never come into my life!' And she turned and started to stride away up the sloping beach, but Blake caught her arm and pulled her round to face him.

'All right, so give me your version of what happened.'

'Why the hell should I? You've already made up your mind so you wouldn't believe me anyway.' Vainly she tried to pull herself free. 'Let me go, damn you. God, how I hate you!' Then stupidly, she found herself held in his arms as she began to sob with rage and frustration.

Raising her tear-filled eyes, she said earnestly, 'I thought there was a shark behind you. I was going to try to hit it if it attacked you.' For some inexplicable reason it suddenly seemed important that he should believe her.

Putting his hands on either side of her face, Blake gently drew her towards him and she felt a wild surge of emotion as she thought that he was going to kiss her again. Her mind told her to break free, but something held her quiet beneath his hands. There was a strange light in his eyes as he looked deeply into hers, as if searching for something he wanted desperately to find. Then he gave a little sigh and dropped his hands to her shoulders. 'I know. I'm sorry.'

A queer feeling of something like disappointment filled her, but she had no time to dwell on it because

Blake was saying briskly, 'We'd better try and dry out our clothes as much as possible before the sun goes down. If you find yourself a bush you can bring your things out to me and I'll wring them out and then spread them to dry.'

He had already begun to unbutton his shirt as Tansy found a clump of pandanus palms, graceful, pretty trees with long aerial roots that made them look as if they were growing upside down, but which formed a screen while she took off her clothes. Her bra and panties she wrung out as best she could and put on again. Luckily they were of nylon and would soon dry in the heat of the sun. Feeling strangely shy, although heaven knows her underthings covered her far more than a bikini, she carried her sweater and slacks out to where Blake had already spread his shirt and shorts out on a convenient shrub. Hardly glancing at her, he took the clothes and squeezed out most of the water before hanging them to dry.

'Is there any chance of a boat coming this way?' he asked matter-of-factly.

'Not at this time of the day. But won't your men come to look for you in your boat when they find you haven't returned?'

'Unfortunately they don't know where we are,' Blake reminded her drily. 'And I doubt whether they'd be able to get even the dinghy over that reef even if we could attract their attention with a signal of some sort. Can this island be seen from Aparoa?'

'Only from the mountain or from the highest rooms in the prison. It was seeing it from your office that gave me the idea.'

'That was the charming idea of abandoning me here, I take it?'

'It would have served you right for locking me in that terrible cell!' Tansy retorted hotly, her scanty attire forgotten as she turned to face him.

He looked into her face for a moment, said, 'You're right—it would have done,' and then turned abruptly away. 'I left my belt out on the rocks before I went after you,' he went on. 'I'll swim out and get it. Are there likely to be any sharks in the lagoon?'

'No, they can't get past the reef.'

He waded out and then swam across the lagoon leaving Tansy looking after him as if she couldn't believe her own ears. Had he really said that? And why on earth had he bothered to admit that he had been in the wrong? But she hardly had time to even begin to work out the implications before he was back. Spreading the belt out on the sand, he undid a leather pouch attached to it and took out a waterproof bag.

'Emergency pack,' he explained, taking things out of it one by one. 'Matches, so that we can light a fire to try to attract attention; water-purifying tablets, a fishing hook and line, a miniature torch, and various pills designed to keep your strength up for about a week.'

'Very impressive,' Tansy said rather sarcastically. 'Any little Boy Scout would be quite proud of it.'

Blake smiled wryly. 'Why don't you go and collect whatever wood you can find to make up a fire while I find a suitable place to build it?'

'You don't need wood,' she informed him with some satisfaction. 'We always light fires of coconut fibre, and you don't have to look for it because the crabs have already collected it for you.'

'The crabs?' He sounded startled.

'Look, I'll show you.' Tansy led him to where a heap of coconut fibres lay in a cleft in the sand. Gently she pushed the heap aside to reveal a small, round hole. 'The sand crabs use the fibre to disguise their holes from the birds,' she explained, 'and you can easily collect all you need.'

They soon gathered armfuls of the material and Tansy followed Blake to the highest point facing Aparoa where he had chosen to light the fire. As she walked behind him her professional eye noted that the wounds on his back were healing well. He walked easily, his muscular legs carrying him effortlessly over the broken terrain. Dressed as he was, in only his short pants, he was a perfect example of physical fitness and forceful masculinity.

Silently she stood and watched him as he went to light the fire, but the match merely sputtered and died, as did the second and third that he tried. Ruefully he looked up and said, 'I'm afraid some damp must have got into them. We'll have to dry them out and then start again.' He spread some of the matches on a stone, but Tansy looked doubtfully at the sun which was sinking low on the horizon, fearing that there wouldn't be enough warmth left to dry them.

Suddenly she wanted to get away from the atoll quickly, away from Blake and her awareness of him. 'I'll try and light it like the natives do,' she volunteered. Searching under the trees she found two pieces of softwood, and taking them back to the pile of fibre began to rub them against each other. After several minutes a little wisp of smoke came from the wood as she manipulated them ever faster, then they began to glow and soon the wood began to smoulder and she was able to hold them close to the coconut fibre until it sprang into flames. Exhausted, she sank back, her hands and arms throbbing from her exertions.

'Well done,' Blake congratulated. 'I'll gather some more fuel.'

They kept the fire burning brightly, but hope gradually

began to die as the sunset faded into a haze of soft
lavender and her eagerly searching eyes could see no
trace of any approaching boat or canoe.

'They won't come now,' she said at last, her voice
empty. 'It's too dark.'

'Yes,' Blake agreed. 'I'm afraid you're right. It looks
as if we shall have to spend the night here.'

# CHAPTER EIGHT

THE atoll was a small, horseshoe-shaped piece of land that had gradually emerged as the coral growth covered an underwater volcanic peak, the highest point of which was only fifteen or twenty feet higher than sea level, so there was little to protect them from the wind from the south which swept up from the Antarctic.

Tansy shivered as the warmth went out of the sun, and Blake, noticing this, said, 'Our clothes should be almost dry now,' and handed her her sweater and slacks which he had put near the fire to finish drying. 'We'd better find something to eat before the light goes,' he remarked as he buckled on his belt, fully dressed again now. 'There obviously isn't any water here, but if we can find something to put it in, I can purify some seawater.'

'I think I'd rather stick to coconut milk,' Tansy said wryly. 'Look, there are several nuts under that tree.'

They found two or three young nuts that sounded as if they had milk in them when shaken, and also some wild bananas which were green but edible, and these they carried back to the fire. Blake drew his knife from the sheaf on his belt and cut a branch from a tree to make into a fishing rod.

'How many fish can you eat?' he asked.

'What makes you think you're going to catch any?' Tansy returned.

He grinned but didn't bother to answer, going down to the lagoon to wade in and cast the line with a crab as bait. Tansy turned her attention to the bananas which she wrapped in leaves and then put in the outer embers of the fire to bake. Finding a piece of jagged coral, she skilfully split the coconuts, being careful not to lose the precious liquid. It reminded her of when she had been a child and she and Ruari had gone exploring Aparoa together, relying for their food on what they could gather from the jungle.

Blake came back with two good-sized fish and soon the delicious smell of cooking food and wood-smoke made Tansy feel less cold and vulnerable. For she was very much alive to the fact that she and Blake were alone together on the tiny island. For the moment they had called a tacit truce, but not far below the surface lay the antagonism and barely suppressed hatred that she felt towards him. But overriding this was her awareness of him as a man, of his strength and forcefulness, of his easy command of the situation. She realised that if she had succeeded in abandoning him on the island he would have suffered no more than a little indignity, a mere prick to his ego, for he had proved that he was quite capable of taking care of his creature comforts.

Across the flickering firelight she looked at his lean, hard profile as he fashioned pieces of flat wood into plates for them. This man, this stranger, who had come to overturn her ordered and sheltered world—he had the ability to rouse her to rage and fury, but he also aroused other emotions in her, feelings more intense than she had ever known before and which made her afraid because they threatened to overpower her reason and make her wonder what it would be like if he again kissed her as he had kissed her once before on the beach at Aparoa. Then he had let her go as soon as she had started to struggle. But then there had been houses and people nearby; here, on the coral atoll, they were alone with no one within call to help her if she needed it—if she wanted it.

As if aware of her regard, Blake raised his head and looked at her, but Tansy picked up a stick and poked the fire, avoiding his eyes and glad of the gathering dusk that hid the slight flush in her cheeks. 'I think the fish should be ready now, don't you?'

'Mm, they look done.' Blake hooked out the fish and put them on the makeshift plates together with the un-wrapped bananas. 'Those smell good, but why bother to cook them?' He spoke quite matter-of-factly, as if they were having a Sunday afternoon picnic.

'They're really plantains, they don't taste as good as cultivated bananas and the natives always bake them.'

He passed her a coconut and Tansy forgot everything but her hunger and thirst. At last, like a kitten, she licked her fingers clean and said, 'That was good. I didn't real-ise I was so hungry.'

'A banquet,' Blake agreed. 'Almost as good as the feast last night.' He looked at her across the firelight, one eyebrow raised mockingly.

His words brought all the memories of last night and the events since then flooding back, she also remembered how he had gone off into the jungle with Lait. She said stiffly, 'I'll wash the plates,' and took them down to the gently lapping water's edge to rinse.

Taking her time, she washed the wooden platters and then sat on the beach to watch the last light of day fade into night. She felt totally unable to cope with her own emotions, rather like a child who is frightened by some-thing but too fascinated to run away, and she bitterly re-sented the unrest that Blake had evoked in her. At last the cool breeze drove her back to seek the warmth of the fire where she found that Blake had taken his pistol from the holster on his belt and was carefully checking to make sure it was still in working order.

Tansy watched him for a few minutes, then said irritably, 'Do you have to do that? We're hardly likely to be attacked by hordes of marauding savages!'

He glanced across at her, then closed the pistol and said evenly, 'Not if it annoys you.' After replacing the gun in his holster, he turned back to look at her. 'What's the matter, Tansy?'

'Matter? What should be the matter? It's just my idea of heaven to be stuck all night on an uninhabited atoll with a—with a tin soldier!' There was a hard, sarcastic edge to her voice.

His brow darkened. 'That's what you think of me, isn't it? That my work is just one long game? Will nothing get it through that crazy head of yours that I'm in deadly earnest?'

'No!' Tansy retorted. 'Like you said, it's just a game —a game played by boys who haven't grown up into men!'

Immediately she had said it she knew that she had gone too far, but something inside her had driven her on into goading him, into trying to break his iron self-control. Blake stood up precipitately, his eyes staring down into hers while Tansy sat frozen, unable to move. Then he bent and picked up a coconut shell and walked a few feet away to where some shrubs gave a little shelter from the wind, and kneeling down began to vigorously scoop away some of the sand.

Tansy bit her lip, knowing that he had every right to be angry with her. Slowly she got up and walked over to him. 'What are you doing? Can I help?' As a peace offering it wasn't much, but he accepted it all the same.

'I'm digging out a hollow for us to sleep in. It should

give a little protection from the wind. If you want to help you can take my knife and cut some leaves to pull over us.'

By the time she returned with an armful of palm and pandanus leaves, Blake had almost finished making a hollow about four feet wide and a foot deep with a banked-up wall around the edges. Tansy looked at it, then said carefully, 'That's fine. Where are you going to put the other one? On the other side of the fire?'

He looked up. 'What other one?'

'One for you and one for me.'

Turning back to his task, he said evenly, 'This one is for both of us. We'll keep warmer if we're together.'

Very clearly, Tansy said, 'Well, that's just where you're wrong!'

'Be sensible, Tansy. It's going to be hard enough to keep warm even with the fire going. If we ...'

Her voice rising, Tansy interrupted angrily, 'I wouldn't sleep in the same hollow as you if you—if you were the last man on earth!'

Raising an eyebrow he grinned in amusement, and she realised how ridiculous her words had sounded. 'You wouldn't get a chance—you'd get killed in the rush,' he said with a chuckle. But then, his voice becoming serious, he added quietly, 'You have nothing to fear from me, Tansy.'

Her arms full of the fresh-smelling leaves, she looked down at him and knew that it was true, but some demon inside her drove her to say tauntingly, 'Oh, I know *that*, Major. I'm fully aware that your tastes run to native girls like Lait!' But it didn't appear to annoy him at all, for he merely grinned again, a broad grin that lit up his face and made her heart lurch, so she added viciously, 'But if you don't mind, Major, I'll make up my own bed.

After all, I do *know* where you've been!'

Dropping the leaves, she picked up another shell and began to dig away at the sand on the other side of the fire, several yards from him. But she was tired and had hardly made much more than an indentation in the sand before she gave up the attempt and crawled into it, pulling some leaves over her as a covering. Vaguely she heard Blake building up the fire, but had already fallen asleep before the moon had risen to turn the tiny islet into an iridescent pearl in the ocean.

Tansy dreamt that she was back in the prison cell, because it was dark and she was cold, so cold. She wrapped her arms round herself, but there was a rustling sound and she thought it was the rat again. Her skin pricked with fear as something touched her foot and suddenly she was sitting up on the sand, screaming. 'The rat! It's a rat!' Her breath came in great sobs and she shuddered with revulsion as something ran across her ankles.

Instantly a torch snapped on and Blake was by her side. 'Tansy, what is it?'

'The rat from the prison cell, it ran across my foot again.' Burying her face in her hands, she began to shake uncontrollably.

Blake moved away, the torch sweeping the ground near her feet, then he was back and was forcibly pulling her hands away. 'No, Tansy, look. Look!' he commanded. 'It was only the crabs. Do you see them?'

Slowly she opened her eyes and saw half a dozen small pink crabs scuttling away from the beam of the torch. 'Crabs! Is that all?' She began to laugh rather hysterically and it was several minutes before she could control herself and realised that Blake was holding her. Quickly she pulled away from him. 'I'm all right now,' she said stiffly.

Softly he said, 'You've had one hell of a day, haven't you?'

Tansy sat up straight. 'And whose fault is that?' she asked tartly.

'Your own. You shouldn't go around stealing my explosives.' His voice had hardened with hers.

'I'm sorry I disturbed you, Major. It won't happen again.' She lay back on the sand and tried to pull the leaves over her.

His eyes glittered angrily in the dark. 'Tansy . . .'

'Yes?' Her eyes challenged his.

Whatever he had been about to say, he changed his mind and said instead, 'You are the most stubborn, mule-headed woman I have ever had the misfortune to meet. When are you going to learn to be sensible?'

But Tansy had already turned her back on him, and, after a few moments, she heard him return to his make-shift bed. The breeze had changed to a cold wind, its icy fingers reaching through her clothes to set her teeth chattering no matter how hard she tried to stop them. Only by stuffing her fingers in her mouth could she keep them silent, but then her arms were so cold that she had to rub them and her teeth began to chatter again violently.

Behind her she heard a muttered imprecation, and two seconds later she was picked up and carried across to his hollow where Blake dropped her willy-nilly. Then he was beside her, pulling the leaves over them. His arms came round her; one to act as her pillow, the other to draw her back against the hard, warm curve of his body. 'Now for God's sake be quiet and let's get some sleep, woman,' he said roughly.

Tansy didn't answer, but she didn't try to get away. Gradually the warmth came back and she wriggled so that his shirt buttons didn't press into her spine. His arms tightened momentarily and she could feel his heart beating against her shoulder blade. 'Major?' she said tentatively.

'Mm?' He sounded half asleep.

'There—there was something I wanted to ask you.'

He sighed, his breath ruffling her hair. 'What is it?'

'When I told you it would serve you right if I'd left you here alone, you said, "Yes, it would have done". What did you mean by that?'

His voice, when he spoke, sounded tired, but not from lack of sleep. 'I didn't intend you ever to go in that cell. I thought you'd take one look at it and refuse to go anywhere near it. It was a ruse, you see, a bluff to make you tell me where the bulldozer part was. But I should have realised that your stubborn pride wouldn't ever let you give in to me.' His hand came up and gripped her shoulder painfully. 'Then I thought for sure that you would only be in there for a few minutes before begging to be let out of that hell-hole. The sergeant was outside the door all the time, waiting to open it at the slightest sound. I got hold of Tupuhoe so fast he didn't know what had hit him. I thought that immediately he saw you in there he would give me the part and let you out, but that wonderful old man is as pig-headed as you are. We just sat there—for hours—waiting for one of us to break, while you ...' He stopped, his voice jagged, his fingers tightening on her shoulder until she winced. 'So now you know. You called my bluff and I came darn near to losing that particular battle. I was about to order the sergeant to let you out when you started screaming.'

'So that's something else I have to thank the rat for,' Tansy said wryly.

'Which rat are you referring to—the animal or the human variety?'

She smiled slightly in the darkness, then, 'Major, I . . .'

But he wouldn't let her finish. 'Not now. Go to sleep.' And he moved his arm to encompass her again.

His confession—for what else could it be called coming from a man as hard as he?—had given her a great deal to think about. But not now; now she was too tired and comfortable to keep awake. Tansy nestled deeper into his arms and heard him give a little grunt deep in his throat before she drifted off to sleep.

She awoke to the sun hot on her back. Woke to a gleaming, dazzling world, a peaceful sun-warmed vista that made the long night seem as if it had never been. Remembering where she was, she sat up hurriedly, but of Blake there was no visible sign, only the indentation of his body in the sand so close to hers. A plume of smoke drifted lazily into the sky from the fire which he had relit, and Tansy stood up to look for him, shaking the white sand from her hair and clothes. Then he came striding along the beach towards her, a couple of fish dangling from his hand.

'Good morning. I trust you approve of fish for breakfast?' He was barefoot, his hair still wet where he had obviously been for a swim.

'That sounds fine.' Tansy tried to speak lightly, but she couldn't help feeling self-conscious about their recent enforced intimacy.

'Good. It will be ready in ten minutes if you want to go for a swim.'

He busied himself over the fire and she slipped gratefully away to strip off her clothes and dive into the soft waters of the lagoon, there to explore the bewilderingly lovely garden of coral beneath the surface. When she returned to Blake her face was bright and glowing. She sniffed the air hungrily. 'I could eat a horse!'

He looked pained. I *did* ask you if fish was all right.

If you'd said you wanted a horse I would have got you one.'

Tansy chuckled and dropped to the sand as she took the platter he held out to her.

Blake glanced up at the column of smoke rising high into the air above them. 'Do you think they'll see that from Aparoa?'

'I should think so. They'll be on the look-out now, anyway.'

And almost before they had finished eating, Tansy heard the throb of the army boat's engines as it sped across the sea towards them. Strangely, she felt a sudden reluctance to return to Aparoa; to return to the knowledge that the man beside her was her hated enemy, who was determined to destroy all that she held dear. Although he still had to find the dynamite, she reminded herself. But even that thought gave her little comfort, for she knew that it would only delay the inevitable, not stop it completely.

Sadly she looked at the approaching boat, but her eyes opened wide as she heard Blake, who had also risen to watch it, say casually, 'You realise that we'll have to get married now, don't you?'

Keeping her voice light, Tansy replied, 'I'd no idea you held such old-fashioned notions, Major. I think my reputation will survive a night spent alone with you.'

Raising his eyebrows, he said mockingly, 'My dear Dr Harland, I wasn't thinking of your reputation—I was thinking of mine!'

The soldiers had brought one of her rowers with them to show them the way over the coral reef for the dinghy and soon they were on board. She caught one or two half-hidden grins from the men, but a look from Blake soon wiped them away.

As soon as they were on their way back, the sergeant

turned to Blake and said triumphantly, 'We've found the explosives, sir. They were hidden in a couple of caves on the mountain. Some youngsters set off a few detonator caps and the sound led us to it.'

Blake shot Tansy a quick look, but said evenly, 'Well done, Sergeant. I take it it's now safely under lock and key?'

'Yes, sir. With a double guard.'

'Were any of the youngsters hurt?' Tansy asked tone- lessly.

'No, miss. It just frightened the wits out of them.' The sergeant's voice wasn't without sympathy, but she turned and looked out across the water feeling miserable inside. So it had all been for nothing, after all—their planning, the feast, the careful choice of hiding place. What had it all added up to? They had delayed the work for only one day.

Half the village seemed to be waiting on the jetty and beach when they sailed into the harbour and eager hands reached out to help her out of the boat and draw her towards the road. At the first of the houses Tansy stopped and glanced back. Blake was standing on the jetty, looking after her. For a long moment she stood there, then turned and went with her fellow islanders.

Within half an hour of their return Tansy could hear the raucous roar of the bulldozer engine as it moved ever nearer to the coconut plantation. Going first to Tupu- hoe's house, she commiserated with the old man and promised to send a radio message to Ruari telling him it was safe to return. At her own house, Inara was wait- ing for her with avid curiosity, but Tansy shrugged off her questions as she changed her clothes.

'How is the young officer?' she asked instead. 'Have you been looking after him?'

'Yes, but he is not a good patient, that one. Last night

he wanted me to give him some crutches, but I say no, not until Doctor Tansy comes back.'

'I promised him I'd take his stitches out today. I'd better go and do it now before he starts fretting.'

When she reached the clinic she found John already sitting in a chair by the window; he had a magazine in his hands but flung this aside as soon as Tansy came in. 'I heard you were back. Everyone was really worried when Blake didn't turn up last night. At first I was afraid that he'd been kidnapped, so I sent the men out searching, but then we realised that you were missing too, so I thought that . . .' he stopped abruptly and looked away from her.

'Yes,' Tansy said slowly, her colour heightening, 'I can imagine just what you thought! If you'll give me your arm I'll help you back to bed so that I can take out your stitches. Then I think you might as well join your comrades in the old prison today instead of waiting until tomorrow,' she added tartly.

'Look, Tansy, I'm sorry,' John said awkwardly as she supported him across to the bed. 'I didn't mean to imply . . .'

'Didn't you?' she asked evenly.

'Well, all right, perhaps I did. But Blake can have almost any woman he wants; he's that type of man. But I didn't want him to add you to the list. You're—sort of special—a friend.' He looked up at her earnestly as he tried to make her understand.

Tansy looked at him for a moment and then gave a slight smile. 'All right, I accept your apology. And for your information nothing happened between us. He's still Enemy Number One as far as I'm concerned, and if the canoe hadn't overturned we would never have got stuck on the atoll.' She turned to wash her hands and prepare her instruments. 'Does Blake have that reputation, then? As a womaniser?' she asked casually.

'Not really. It's mostly women who get attracted to him, but I've never heard of him showing more than a passing interest in anyone. There was one officer's wife I heard about who ...'

But Tansy found that she didn't want to hear. 'Lie still now while I take your stitches out,' she interrupted quickly.

Dressed in white coat and surgical mask, she concentrated on her task, but almost dropped the tweezers she was holding as a loud explosion shook the thin walls of the building.

'What on earth was that?'

John looked at her unhappily. 'Dynamite. Blake must have started widening the gap in the reef. I expect he'll really push on with the work now; he's got quite a bit of time to make up.'

And push on he did, for later in the morning, after Tansy had seen John safely transferred to the prison, a young native boy ran to tell her that the soldiers were about to cut down the first of the coconut palms. A large crowd of people had collected on the plateau to watch, and Tansy slipped through them to stand at Tupuhoe's side. The soldiers looked uneasily at the natives so that the sergeant looked towards Blake, who was standing by the jeep, his face quite devoid of any emotion. He nodded briefly and the sergeant ordered the men to continue.

The whirr of a rotary saw filled the silence as they cut through the first tree. The great palm broke loose and almost imperceptibly started to fall with a great tearing groan of sound. Mortally wounded, the tree twisted like a man who had been shot, then fell crashing to the ground in a cloud of dust. Then the men moved on to the next palm as the bulldozer effortlessly uprooted the stump of the once proud tree. For a little while longer they watched before Tansy led Tupuhoe gently away. The old man seemed to have aged greatly in the last few days; his back was no longer as straight as it had been and there were lines of sadness in his face. Tansy was filled with a fierce gladness that they had tried to fight the soldiers, however unavailing their efforts. Tupuhoe would have that, at least, to look back on with pride amidst the depth of his unhappiness.

The jeep overtook them as they walked down the hill; going down to the harbour to supervise the work there, Tansy supposed. It seemed that Blake couldn't get the job done fast enough, for all day long the noise of demolition continued, only to cease when it was too dark to carry on with safety. And at first light the next morning, although it was Sunday, the machines started up again. He drove his men on relentlessly, so that by the time Tansy emerged from her afternoon clinic half the plantation had disappeared.

That evening she spent at Tupuhoe's house, for Ruari had returned and wanted to know all that had happened in his absence. He was furiously angry at Blake's treatment of them and it took much persuasion from Tupuhoe and Lait, who was also there, to stop him from going to the prison there and then. Tansy, however, took little part in the conversation, content to let the others do the talking. They sat on the darkened veranda, only a lamp inside the house giving a mellow light through the window. Grey clouds scudded across the face of the moon and then it began to rain; hissing, pelting drops that bounced fiercely off every surface, turning the dusty road into a muddy stream within minutes. Ruari and Tupuhoe went to see to their livestock while Tansy and Lait sat together to watch the rainstorm end as suddenly as it had begun.

'It was a good job we didn't have the feast today,' Tansy remarked. 'It would have been washed away in that downpour.'

Lait laughed. 'Also it would have made the jungle floor very wet!'

Tansy didn't answer, remembering just who Lait had taken into the jungle that night.

As if guessing her thoughts, Lait continued, 'He is one strange man, that officer. While we sit at the feast I teach him the kiss of Aparoa, with lips to the forehead and then nose against nose, and he seems to like this and to like me. But when I lead him into the jungle and find a good place he wants only to talk. He asks me about you and about Ruari. Always he wants talk, not make kiss. Then he says he must look to see if the young officer is all right and we go back to the feast. Then, when he sees that you have taken the young officer to the clinic, he says he must return to the prison and he leaves me behind. Why you think he does this, Tansy?'

'I—I can't think,' Tansy replied, but she remembered Blake's broad grin when she had accused him of preferring native girls. Had he done it deliberately to get under her skin? To make her—jealous? But why should he think that she could possibly be jealous when he knew that she hated and despised him? Because she had told him so often enough, hadn't she?

The air was filled with that washed-clean aroma that always came after a long time without rain and the scents of the jungle stole out to fill the night, as she walked slowly home with Ruari by her side. He reached up and broke off a delicate, deep-pink hibiscus blossom and gave it to her to put in her hair, little drops of moisture still clinging to the petals. Tansy automatically put it in the left side to show that she had no sweetheart and didn't notice the quizzical look in Ruari's eyes.

'I'm worried about your father,' she told him. 'It isn't doing him any good to be here at the moment. Can't you take him away to visit your relations on one of the other islands for a while?'

Ruari shrugged, a quite un-nativelike gesture. 'I don't think he would go. He wants to be with the people, which is understandable. If his asthma gets worse I'll try to persuade him to go, but I'm afraid he won't listen.'

'Well, I'll keep an eye on him, of course, but his strength seems to have diminished rapidly lately,' Tansy sighed.

They talked for a little while longer before Tansy entered the house and went to bed, fully expecting to wake to the sound of the saw cutting through the remaining palms. But instead she was jerked into wakefulness by the jangling sound of the emergency bell attached to the radio and hurried downstairs to take the message while Inara went running to rouse her rowers. Soon she was scudding across the sea, the sail billowing in the moonlight, to attend a woman with a difficult childbirth, the destruction behind her, her only worry that she might not be in time. Quite often the native midwives would leave calling her until the last minute and she would arrive too late to help the patient, but this time the woman had been sensible and she got there in time to save both mother and child.

While on the island, which was about a quarter the size of Aparoa, she decided to stay on for another couple of days to check the health of the inhabitants and arranged to take back with her an intelligent youth of about fourteen to whom she could teach the rudiments of first-aid and nursing in the hope that he would be able to deal with many of the minor ailments—a policy which her father had started and they found very useful.

When she returned this time, the view of Aparoa from the sea was vastly different, the ranks of dancing palms having gone completely. Strangely, only the small knoll with its crown of jungle trees where she loved to sit still stood. Beyond it stretched a long, unbroken area of open land that would soon lie under thousands of tons of concrete and be heavy with the noise of planes. The gap into the harbour was much wider now, large enough to admit quite a big boat, and the lagoon beyond less calm and peaceful as the ocean waves met less opposition and came thundering down on to the beach.

The rest of the day passed busily as Tansy arranged accommodation for the youth she had brought back, dealt with patients who had turned up at the clinic, and then went on her rounds. Inara had cooked her a delicious supper of roast fish served with breadfruit, and after it Tansy sat for a long time in her father's chair in his study, gazing silently out at the changed landscape. The day turned to dusk, but she didn't bother to put on the light. Then, when the sun was soon to slip below the horizon in its eternal circle, she went quietly past the kitchen where Inara sang at her work, and slipped into the garden. Slowly she went along the familiar path between the aromatic plants that filled the night with a potpourri of scents, past the tinkling waterfall and up the hill to the plateau.

She looked back along the deserted strip of land, the fallen trees cleared, the holes where they had stood filled in, and then lifted her head in puzzlement. It was a few seconds before she realised what was wrong; she could no longer hear the singing of the palm leaves as they danced in the breeze. They were dead and gone for ever. Turning, she made her way to the knoll and walked under the trees until she came to the cliff's edge, there to lean against a trunk and watch the sun sink into the sea.

It was so quiet that she heard him coming from quite a distance away. He made no attempt to hide his approach, but she didn't turn round to look at him until Blake was standing just a few feet away from her. He looked different somehow, and then she saw that he wasn't wearing his uniform. Instead he wore navy slacks and shirt, open at the throat and betraying a hint of a hairy chest, with the cuffs turned back casually. It was the first time she had ever seen him in civilian clothes and they made him look leaner and even more powerful.

'How did you know where to find me?' she said slowly into the silence.

'If I tell you you'll probably accuse me of spying or voyeurism.' There was an ironic twist to his mouth as he answered.

Rather unsteadily, she said, 'Why don't you try me?'

He paused, then, 'All right. The first night I met you, after you'd told me just what you thought of me and my kind, I didn't go straight back to the prison, but wandered up this way. You walked right by me on your way here. I wondered if you were in the habit of going out alone at night, so I waited the next night. When you came again I decided I'd better keep an eye on you, so, whenever you went out alone, I followed you.'

'So it was you who shouted after me when I swam out too far. And that's why you were on hand when the soldier attacked me,' Tansy said on a note of understanding.

'Yes.'

'Why did you follow me?'

'Because I didn't want any harm to come to you.'

'After what I'd said to you? After I'd done my best to get you to go away? Why should you care what happens to me?'

His voice changed as he said roughly, 'I care.'

Tansy straightened up and moved a little towards him so that she could see his face. His eyes looked intently down at her, a light in them that she couldn't fail to understand.

'Why here?' She spoke almost in a whisper. 'Why not when we were alone together on the atoll?'

'Because then you could have accused me of trying to take advantage of the situation. Here you're free to walk away—if you want to,' he added deliberately.

Her heart beating wildly, Tansy stared up at him. 'I hate you, you know that!'

'Do you, Tansy? Do you really?' He had moved closer and reached out to take the clip from her hair so that it fell in cascades of silver about her shoulders.

'You're a soldier, and I loathe war and violence,' she went on hurriedly.

'But there's a man under the uniform, and it's the man that matters.' Gently he began to stroke the side of her face, his touch as light as butterflies' wings.

Tansy began to quiver, her breath uneven. 'I despise you and everything you stand for,' she managed.

'Methinks the lady doth protest too much,' he quoted softly as his fingers slipped down to explore her throat, warm, caressing.

Closing her eyes, she gave a half-hearted protest that somehow changed to a little moan. Then she opened her eyes. 'Blake! Oh, Blake!'

The next second she was almost swept off her feet as

he engulfed her in his arms, his mouth finding hers as he kissed her with a violence that terrified her and yet aroused emotions within her that she didn't know existed. With a choking sob, she thrust herself even closer to him and passionately returned his kiss. When eventually Blake raised his head, his breathing was heavy and uneven, his eyes glazed. He held her tight in his arms and Tansy could hear his heart hammering in his chest.

'Oh, my darling.' His voice was slurred and unsteady, hardly recognisable. 'I've been waiting so long for you to call me by my name. I knew that when at last you did it would be because you'd realised what I've known all along.'

She stirred and pulled away to look at him wonderingly, her hand reaching tentatively up to touch the planes of his face, to brush his lips. He gave a kind of groan and turned his head to press his lips into her palm.

'My lovely girl, if you knew how long I've searched for someone like you.' He drew her towards him and bent his head to kiss her eyes, her cheekbones, and then hungrily sought her lips again, kissing her like a thirst-crazed man who has found water and cannot get his fill.

At last they drew apart and Tansy gazed mistily up at him. 'I've been trying so hard to fight this. I wouldn't even let myself think of you as a man, only as my enemy. But I should have known it was inevitable. All the time I had to keep telling myself how much I hated you; even after you kissed me on the beach I wouldn't let myself admit how much I liked it, how much I wanted you to do it again.'

'Crazy little idiot,' he said thickly, and proceeded to do just that, very thoroughly.

Later Tansy somehow found herself sitting on the grass beside him, her head pillowed against his shoulder. 'What did you mean when you said you'd known all along?'

He smiled. 'I was completely bowled over on that first night when I pulled you out into the moonlight and took that ridiculous turban off your head. You've no idea how lovely you looked at that moment. That's why I didn't go straight back to the prison; I had to recover from what had hit me.' Gently he ran his fingers through her hair, curling it round his fingers. 'You were in a flaming temper at the time, of course. That's probably what did it,' he said with laughter in his voice. 'But then I've hardly ever seen you in anything *but* a flaming temper.'

Tansy smiled in the darkness, knowing the power she had over him. 'I'm not in a temper now,' she said softly.

His fingers tightened in her hair. 'No,' he said unevenly. 'So you're not.' And this time when the embrace ended it was by his act, not hers. 'You know, Dr Harland, you're quite a girl.' He cupped her face in his hands and his dark eyes, lit by a light that was for her alone, looked deep into hers. 'Tansy, I want to take you with me when I leave here. Will you come with me, my darling?'

She knew what he asked of her, knew that it would mean leaving everything she had ever loved, but it didn't matter, not beside the feelings he had awakened in her.

'Yes, Blake,' she said simply. 'I'll come with you.'

The sudden flare of emotion in his eyes disconcerted her. She had fallen in love with a complete, complex stranger, and as yet she had caught only glimpses of the depth of feeling of which he was capable.

'Oh, my beautiful, wonderful girl,' he said in a curious, wrenched voice. 'I've waited so long for you. I want you and need you so much.'

Tansy found that she was crying. 'I love you,' she whispered. 'I'll always love you.'

Gently he laid her back on the grass to kiss her again, his lips caressing her until his mouth became possessive, demanding, and his hands began to explore her body.

The singing of the wind in the coconut palms had gone for ever, but instead there was the music of the waves sliding over the sand, and above them a full moon shed its brilliance over the island; an immense moon that turned from silver to pale green, showering a pathway of diamonds and turning the sea to molten silver as the day passed into eternity.

# CHAPTER NINE

THE sun was already high in the sky when Tansy finally awoke the next morning, but she didn't rush to jump out of bed as she normally would have done. Instead she turned over to stare at the beamed ceiling, her eyes bright and her mouth curved into a smile of happiness. She was in love with Blake—so few words to describe the most momentous thing that would ever happen in her life. For from this moment nothing would ever be quite the same again; for the rest of her life there would be someone else whose happiness would mean more to her than her own. Dreamily she lay there as she recalled every detail of the previous night. She had known instinctively when she saw the knoll still intact that he had left it there for her sake and that if she went there he would come to her. And, although her mind had rebelled, her heart had led her there to wait for him.

Then she remembered that they were meeting again today, so she jumped quickly out of bed and ran downstairs. Inara was in the kitchen and Tansy breathlessly asked her to prepare a picnic for two before taking her usual bathe under the waterfall.

Inara smiled knowingly at her when she came back, but Tansy didn't care. Hurrying upstairs to put on a pretty summer dress, she turned towards the mirror with a hairbrush in her hand, and then stopped short—she looked so different! Her eyes sparkled brighter than any jewel and there was a radiance about her that enhanced her delicate loveliness. She positively glowed! And all because a man has told me he loves me, she thought happily. Well, no, that wasn't quite right, because he hadn't actually said it, not in so many words, but he had certainly demonstrated, very convincingly, how he felt about her. And she was to leave Aparoa and go with him, be his wife. But he hadn't said that either, now she came to think of it. But it didn't matter; there was plenty of time—they had all the time in the world.

Blake picked her up just before noon and they drove deep into the heart of the island, away from the villages, and left the jeep on the valley road while they walked to a sunlit clearing in the jungle near to a small lake adorned by giant lily pads. He wore civilian clothes again, beige slacks and a matching loose-knit shirt, as if he had left the soldier behind at the prison. Suddenly Tansy felt shy of this big stranger who was capable of arousing feelings in her that frightened her by their depth and passion. Spreading a rug for them to sit on, he turned and held out his hand to her, but she hung back a little.

Sensing her need for reassurance, he crossed to her and said in mock complaint, 'Do you realise you haven't kissed me all morning?' and bent his head to find her mouth, to cover her lips with little kisses that intoxicated her and left her clinging to him weakly when at last he released her.

Scooping her up, he carried her across to the rug and dropped her gently down on to it. 'Come on, wench, I'm hungry. Where's the food?'

Tansy wrinkled her nose at him. 'Just like a man! All you care about is filling your stomach.'

He grinned as he dropped down beside her. 'One must get one's priorities right from the start,' he told her teasingly. 'If you don't hurry up and unpack that hamper I shall have to start on you.' And he leant over to gently bite her earlobe.

Laughingly she turned to push him away—then found herself clinging to him in fear as the ground beneath them began to shake violently. There was a terrible grumbling, groaning sound deep within the earth, a tree came crashing down into the lake, its still waters already overflowing its banks as yet another earth tremor shook the island. The quake lasted only for seconds, but to Tansy it seemed an age before the earth was still at last and Blake released her from the protection of his arms as she raised frightened eyes to look into his.

'It's all right, it's over now. That was some . . .'

'No, it isn't all over! We have to get away, quickly!' Jumping to her feet, she pulled him up beside her and began to run back through the jungle towards the jeep.

'Wait! Tell me what's the matter.' Blake caught hold of her arm and made her stop.

Agitatedly Tansy tried to draw him on. 'It's the *tsunami*. We have to get to higher ground quickly!'

'*Tsunami*?' he repeated in bewilderment. 'What on earth's that?'

'Tidal waves! The seismic disturbances under the sea generate shock waves that make huge waves in the sea, higher than a wall, and they sweep right across the islands destroying everything in their path. Come on, we have to get to the jeep and drive to higher ground before they come. We don't stand a chance here in the valley!'

Grimly Blake took her hand and led the way through the trees, using his shoulders to shelter her from the branches in their way. Soon they were back at the jeep and Tansy thankfully clung to its side as Blake drove at speed towards higher ground, but when they came to a fork in the road he swung the vehicle back towards the main village.

'No, this is the wrong way,' Tansy called out over the noise of the engine. 'The other road leads to the mountain.'

'I've got to get back to my men and warn them,' Blake returned as he gunned the jeep down the track.

'But the villagers will take care of them. They'll be safe in the prison—everyone always shelters there. Please, Blake, there isn't time!'

'You're sure they'll be safe?'

'Yes!'

'All right.' He swung the jeep round in a circle of screaming brakes and plunged up the mountain road.

The jeep was built for rough terrain such as this, but even the jeep couldn't withstand the boulder dislodged from the hillside, that came bouncing and crashing down to crush the radiator. Blake cursed but wasted no time in examining the damage; one look was enough to tell him that the vehicle would take them no further.

'We'll have to run for it.' Taking her hand, he ran her fast up the track. Tansy considered herself to be pretty fit, but the way was steep and she was soon panting for breath as she tried to keep up with him. Blake took her left hand in his and put his right arm round her to help her along and thus make it a little easier.

The road veered off to the right, downhill again, but Tansy, her breath coming in quick gasps, pointed to a tree-lined track that led upwards. Hardly had they started up it, however, before she heard a faint noise in the distance. 'Listen!' She clutched his sleeve and then Blake heard it too. A swishing, rushing noise that gradually became louder, began to grow into a roar.

Desperately they ran on, Blake almost carrying her as

her strength began to fail. But the sound was like thunder now, the mortal groan of trees being uprooted in its path adding to the terrible surging roar. The first giant wave could only be yards away from them now and Tansy knew with a horrifying certainty that they weren't going to make it. Blake, too, must have realised how close it was, for he suddenly swung off the track towards a stout tree. Tansy found herself holding tightly to the trunk and then Blake's arms came round to encircle her and the tree, his hands locked into one another in a grip that couldn't be torn apart while he still had life in his body.

Then the wave was upon them. A great, crashing wall of muddy water that swept their feet from under them and sent branches of trees and debris to knock and bruise them and try to dislodge their hold. For a brain-chilling moment Tansy thought the tree was going to be swept away, but its roots went deep into the ground and it held, but under the immense pressure she lost her hold on the trunk and found herself slipping down within Blake's arms. The sea water cascaded over her head as she tried to regain her grip on the tree, but then his arms tightened as he exerted all his strength against the great force that tried to take them in its giant maw.

When the wave passed at last, Tansy found herself lying entangled in the exposed roots of the tree, the sea having washed away the earth round them. Slowly, numbly, she extricated herself and then looked round for Blake. He was lying a few feet away, on his back, his eyes closed and face deathly white. Tansy gave a little choking cry of fear as she crawled across the muddy ground towards him.

'Blake!' With trembling fingers she felt for his pulse.

He opened his eyes. 'I'm—all right.' But his breath was

ragged and uneven. 'Something hit me. Took the—the wind out of me,' he gasped. Slowly he sat up and rubbed his shoulders; the battle with the wave had almost torn his arms from their sockets. 'Will there be any more waves?' he asked through clenched teeth.

'There might be, but not as big. Are you badly hurt?' she asked anxiously.

'No, it just knocked me out for a bit.' He staggered to his feet and pulled her up beside him. 'We'd better try to get a bit higher.'

Draggingly they started to climb up the track again. The tidal waves came again, twice more, but this time they were well clear and could stand and watch as the mighty torrents of water swept past to die away in the middle of the island, over three miles inland.

'Which is the best way to get back?' Blake asked her grimly.

'If we keep climbing we'll come to a track that runs along the ridge of the mountain and comes out on the plateau above the village. It's a long way, but it will be the safest.'

'The safest? Isn't the danger over now?'

Tansy turned to look at him, her mud-streaked dress starting to dry in the sun. 'No. With all the earth from the valley floor swept away it undermines the higher ground and creates landslides. We have to get above the tree line,' she answered tiredly.

Blake put his arm round her comfortingly. 'We can make it. We haven't survived this far to get killed in a landslide.' He kissed her lightly and then grinned. 'You look terrible!'

Tansy smiled weakly back .'You don't look exactly a fashion plate yourself!'

The next few hours were a nightmare that was to

haunt her for the rest of her life. The going was rough and hard and her legs ached more with every step. Several times they heard an ominous rumbling sound and saw whole slices of the hillside move, slowly at first, and then with gathering momentum to crash and tumble into the valley taking trees and great lumps of rock in their wake. Without Blake she knew she would never have made it. Despite the punishment he had taken, from somewhere he still found the strength and endurance to help and encourage her over the long miles until they came at last to the plateau.

With the trees gone, they had an uninterrupted view of the valley below them, but the familiar landmarks had changed completely in the few short hours since the earthquake. Tansy slid exhaustedly to the ground and just sat and stared, unable to take in the scene of devastation. Of the houses in the village only the few stone buildings, her own house among them, still stood. Of the thatched and wooden houses there was no sign, except for a sheet of corrugated iron that hung perilously from the branches of a high tree, and a few cooking pots still in place where once had been the kitchens of houses.

'The clinic! It's gone!' she exclaimed in dismay. 'All my equipment, everything!'

'We'd better get to the prison. I think I can see some people moving about outside it,' Blake said with worry in his voice. His anxiety for his men spurred him along and when Tansy flagged he simply picked her up and carried her.

Relieved shouts greeted them as the people caught sight of them. Both soldiers and islanders, their enmity forgotten, came running to meet them. Ruari was there first and lifted her from Blake's tired arms to carry her into the prison.

'Thank God you're safe, Tansy. We've all been so worried about you. Are you hurt?'

'No, just exhausted. Oh, Ruari, is everyone all right? Were many hurt?' she asked anxiously.

'Everyone from the village took refuge in the prison. But the other villages . . .' He didn't have to finish; Tansy knew quite well that there were at least three other villages which were in the direct line of the *tsunami*.

John Andrews and the soldiers were crowding around Blake. 'Have you radioed for help yet?' he was asking. 'What about the boat? Sergeant, take two men and see if you can find out what's become of it. John, I want a reconnaissance party sent out to find the extent of the damage to the island. Get the radio operator to send out an emergency message for medical supplies, emergency rations and tents. Tell them they can land light aircraft and helicopters on the plateau. Is the bulldozer still working? Then use it to clear the debris from this road into the valley.'

Within a very short time he was directing the soldiers about a bewildering number of tasks, while the islanders tried to salvage what they could of their belongings. Tansy found that her own house, which was higher up the hill than most of the others, was not too badly damaged; the water had swept through the ground floor and left everything sodden and thick with sand and mud, including the radio transmitter, but the upper storey was completely untouched. Quickly she washed and changed out of her filthy clothes, then set some of the native women to work cleaning the downstairs rooms. With the clinic gone she would have to use the house as a makeshift hospital and knew that when the people caught in the tidal wave started being brought in she would need all the space and beds she could get.

Ruari tried the generator but was unable to make it work, so all through the rest of the day and the long night, as more and more people were brought to her, she had to do her work as best she could by lamp and candlelight. Her own exhaustion pushed firmly to the back of her mind, she used the meagre supply of drugs that she had at the house to give local anaesthetics as she set broken bones, extracted huge splinters and sewed cuts and gashes.

In the early hours Blake came with casks of fresh water, for the river water was now undrinkable. 'I've organised some of the men to refill the casks from the waterfall behind your house,' he told her. 'There's some of our food that we had over from the last shipment, too. I'm afraid the islanders' crops are completely ruined, but this should last until help gets here.'

Tansy finished putting a woman's broken arm into splints; it was all she could do, she had already run out of plaster. 'Did you get a message out?' she asked wearily.

'Yes, they're sending out supplies as soon as they can get them loaded aboard a plane. The Aparoans are making torches to light up a landing path so that it can land safely.'

Tansy looked up at him. He ought to have been flat on his back, but, apart from a rather pallid look about his mouth, he seemed as capable as ever. He had changed into his uniform again and Tansy realised that he had trained for years to cope with emergencies such as this; he knew exactly what had to be done and in what priority, wasn't afraid to make decisions and made sure that they were carried out. She was extremely, thankfully, glad that he was there.

She smiled slightly. 'Why don't you say, I told you so?'

He raised an eyebrow mockingly. 'Now why should I do that?'

'You know very well. You always said we needed an airstrip.'

He grinned, but merely said, 'I'll get the medical supplies to you directly they come in. And I'll send one of my men to try and fix the generator as soon as it's light.' He put a finger under her chin, tilting her face to look into his. 'I know I can't tell you not to overwork yourself, but promise me you'll try to get some rest whenever you can.' He kissed the tip of her nose and went off into the night.

The next three days seemed like one interminably long one as Tansy somehow coped with the never-ending stream of patients. The small aircraft brought her badly needed drugs and came back several times more before it was joined by a helicopter ferrying supplies from a ship out in the bay. The noise of the engines was increased by that of the army boat which had been swept inland, but Blake's soldiers had managed to repair it and put it back into service within a miraculous twenty-four hours. This brought the shocked, bewildered survivors from the smaller, coral islands, many of which had been almost completely engulfed by the huge tidal waves.

Tansy kept herself going with the aid of stimulants, but felt a great, heartfelt surge of relief when, shortly after the plane had landed yet again, she turned round and saw her father standing in the doorway.

'Daddy!' She flung herself into his arms and was held very, very tightly. 'Oh, Daddy, I'm so glad you've come!'

He looked fit and well and she started to question him

eagerly about his trip to Australia, but after one look at her white, drawn face, he ordered her straight to bed. 'Go and get some sleep. Don't worry, I've brought another doctor and a nurse with me. I've lots to tell you, but it can wait until you've had a good, long sleep.'

From then on conditions improved tremendously; the other doctor, a young Australian, took it upon himself to travel round the islands with Ruari as interpreter; the most badly hurt patients were shipped out to be taken to hospital and the number of casualties gradually lessened. Blake and his squad of men continued to work indefatigably at clearing the river and roads, putting up dozens of tents for the homeless, handing out food supplies and, tragically, digging out those who had been buried beneath the landslides.

'I have to hand it to the soldiers,' David Harland remarked as they took a breather out in the garden one afternoon a few days later. 'They may have come here to perform an extremely unpleasant task, but their efforts have certainly minimised the scale of the disaster. That officer certainly knows his job.'

'Yes. Yes, he does.' There were two bright spots of colour in Tansy's cheeks as she added, 'As a matter of fact, Daddy, I wanted to talk to you about that.' As yet they had both been too busy for her to tell him that she intended leaving Aparoa with Blake, and now that the moment had come she felt strangely shy and reluctant, knowing how her father would feel at the thought of losing her.

'And I have something to tell you. Something extremely important,' her father interrupted before she could go on. 'You remember I told you I had met some old friends in Australia? Well, I—er ...' Amazingly her usually self-possessed father seemed strangely embarrassed and unsure of himself as he flushed beneath his tan. 'Well, to be brief, one of them was the widow of an old colleague, and we saw quite a lot of each other and— well, we decided to make a go of it. We intend to be married very quietly as soon as I can return to Sydney,' he finished hurriedly, his face red.

'Daddy!' Tansy stared at him in astonishment. 'But— but that's wonderful news! I'm so happy for you. Tell me all about her,' she commanded. 'What's her name? Has she any children? And when will she be coming to join you on Aparoa?' To Tansy it was indeed wonderful news, for now she would feel far less guilty about leaving him.

David Harland smiled, pleased with her enthusiasm. 'Her name's Evelyn, and yes, she has three children, two married and one at college in Sydney.' Then he looked at her a little uncertainly. 'But that's just it, Tansy. It's because of her children that she doesn't want to leave Australia, so I intend to buy into a practice there just as soon as my contract on Aparoa ends in a couple of months' time.'

Completely stunned by his words, Tansy could only stand and stare at him wordlessly. Seeing the shocked look on her face, he hurried on, 'I know that this has come as a complete surprise to you, my dear, but I've done my best for Aparoa over the last twenty years and now I'm handing over to you. I know how much you love the island, and knowing that you will be here to carry on has given me the fortitude to break from it. I'm too old for all these changes that are taking place, too old to start all over again, but you're young enough to take things in your stride. With Ruari to help you and the boys being educated in Australia coming along, you'll be able to cope far better than I ever could.'

When she still didn't answer he took her slack hands in his and said earnestly, 'Tansy, please try to understand. After your mother's death I shut myself away here, but this last trip to Australia, meeting old friends, catching up on all the things that have been happening in the world, has shown me just how wrong I was. I need them, Tansy. I need Evelyn and I need the home she's willing to make for me. I know how you must feel, but you'll be able to visit us as often as you like. If you hadn't said so many times that you loved Aparoa and never wanted to leave it, then perhaps I might have hesitated, but this is your home and I know how happy you are here.'

Numbly Tansy returned the pressure of his hands and tried to smile. 'Yes, it's all right, I understand. You'll just have to give me a little time to get used to the idea, though.'

He smiled in some relief. 'That's my girl! I knew you wouldn't let me down. In fact I've already submitted your name for my post when I handed in my resignation before I left Canberra. It's only a formality, of course, the authorities are bound to give you the job.'

They turned to walk on together as Dr Harland went on eagerly to tell her about his future wife and her family. To Tansy it seemed that he had already gone from her; he seemed to be more a part of the new life he was so eager to get back to than of her own familiar surroundings, of which he had always been the main part.

The knoll at the top of the cliffs had gone now, bull-dozed out of the way so that the plane could land, so there was no familiar place for Tansy to sit and try to work out her problem after her father had gone back to the house. Slowly she wandered down to the beach and walked along until she found a rock where she could sit with her chin cupped in her hand and stare at the sea. His news had come as such a devastating shock that for a long time she felt too numb to think straight. She loved her father very much and he was happier now than he had been for years; there was a spring in his step and a new, enthusiastic air about him. But Tansy knew that if she told him about Blake he would insist on her leaving with him, would put her happiness before his own. And she knew that she couldn't do that to him. He had suffered enough in his life and deserved whatever happiness and joy he could get for the latter part of his life.

He had said that he knew she wouldn't let him down and Tansy realised that that would mean not leaving Aparoa herself. One of them had to be there to take care of the islanders, especially now, after the double tragedy of losing their livelihoods and their homes. But to stay here would mean losing Blake.

Miserably she tried to think of alternatives, but she was just chasing rainbows; she knew that her father's right to happiness came before her own. It was sunset before she left the beach, a beautiful, glorious sunset of deep orange over flaming purple, that set the sea on fire with colour. With reluctant feet, each step harder to take than the one before, she went slowly up to the prison and asked one of the soldiers to tell Blake that she wanted to see him.

He came at once, his step brisk, an eager light in his eyes as he saw her.

'I hope you didn't mind me coming to see you?'

'I'm glad you did. I've been wondering when you'd be free enough to devote some time to me instead of your patients.' He drew her arm through his and walked her through the trees until they were out of sight of the prison buildings. 'I definitely contemplated cutting my finger or something so that I could get in the queue and at least see you that way.' In a small, quiet clearing where the leaves on the trees turned to silver in the moonlight, he stopped and drew her gently towards him. 'Darling, I've missed you so.' His kiss was gentle at first, but then his lips strayed to her throat, her neck, before returning with fierce insistence to her lips.

Tansy clung to him shamelessly, her body arched against his with desperate yearning. She wanted this moment to go on and on for ever, never wanted it to end. Because when it ended she would have to do the hardest thing she had ever done. Reluctantly he lifted his head at last, his breath ragged, his hand unsteady as he raised it to touch her face wonderingly.

'Tansy, my sweet girl,' he murmured thickly when he had recovered his breath a little. 'I've had orders to leave here in two days. NATO are sending others in to actually build the airstrip now that we've done all we can for the islanders. And now that your father and the other medical staff are here you'll be free to leave with me, won't you? Would you like me to talk to your father?'

'No.' Tansy freed herself from the love and warmth of his arms and stepped away from him. It was the longest, hardest step she had ever taken in her life. 'I'm not coming with you, Blake.' She managed to say it quite firmly, but her heart was torn apart by divided loyalties.

'You mean you can't be spared yet? That's a great disappointment. How long do you think it will be before you can follow me to England?'

Painfully she said, 'I won't be coming at all. I've changed my mind.'

He stared at her for a moment, the silence shattering in its intensity. Then he gripped her arms so tightly that she gave a little cry of pain. 'What are you saying? You can't possibly mean that!'

'I'm—I'm sorry, Blake.' The inadequate words were said in little more than a whisper.

'You're sorry! My God, is that all you can find to say? Why? Something must have happened to make you change your mind. Is it your father? I'll talk to him, tell him that ...'

'No! No, please. It's nothing to do with my father,' she said quickly.

'Then for God's sake, *why*, Tansy?'

She swallowed painfully and said in a trembling voice, 'Because I've realised that I can't leave Aparoa.' She held up a restraining hand when he tried to swiftly interrupt. 'I know I said I would, but after the earthquake, when all the poor injured people were brought in ...' she broke off, then said earnestly, 'I know and understand them, Blake. They're my people and they're going to need me more than ever now.'

'But your father—he can take care of them as well, if not better, than you,' he said urgently.

'My father isn't a young man and there aren't many more years before he retires. I can't leave him to carry on alone.'

He stared down at her, the moon outlining his hard profile. 'You told me you loved me.'

Tansy's nails dug deep into the palms of her clenched fists. 'I know.'

'One doesn't just fall out of love, Tansy.'

'I know that too. That's why this is so hard to say. But I have to say it, Blake,' she added brokenly.

His eyes darkened and there was a note of urgent entreaty in his voice as he said tensely, 'Don't do this to us, Tansy.'

'I have to. I don't have any choice.'

He went to reach out for her, but she moved away, afraid that her shallow resolution would dissolve if he touched her.

'You do have a choice. The islanders managed without you and your father before; let someone else take over now.' There, was a note of anger in his voice as he failed to make her change her mind.

'They need me!'

'And do you think that I don't? My God, Tansy, haven't I *shown* you just how much I need you?' he said savagely.

Chokingly she shook her head. 'No, Blake, you've stood on your own two feet, been in charge of others, for too long ever to be completely dependent on another person for your happiness. And as for your physical needs —well, I'm sure you'll always be able to find plenty of women who'd be more than willing to satisfy those.'

He glared at her, his eyes glittering with barely suppressed fury, his mouth set into a thin, hard line. 'I ought to knock your head off for saying that. The very fact that you can say it at all only proves that you have no conception of how much you mean to me!' And now she saw the look that came down over his face; bleak, bitter pride shutting down over anger.

Breathing heavily, he unbuttoned the pocket of his tunic and pulled out a notepad and pencil. 'Here,' he said after he had written on it. 'This is the address of my club in London. When you come to your senses contact me there and I'll come out and get you.'

With trembling fingers Tansy took it from him. She daren't look up at his face; she knew that if she did the unshed tears that filled her heart would overflow, and she mustn't cry, not yet, not until she was alone with her grief and misery. He walked her to her garden gate, not touching her, a cold brittle silence between them. But he suddenly caught her to him, to kiss her with a desperate, bruising passion. Tansy forced herself not to return it, to stand rigidly within his arms. He raised his head to look into her eyes and then turned abruptly on his heel and marched away, his back ramrod-straight, leaving Tansy standing in the road feeling more alone than she had ever felt in her life.

# CHAPTER TEN

THE soldiers started moving out their equipment the next day and by dawn of the following morning they were gone. Soon their place was taken by soldiers of other NATO countries who began to lay the tons of concrete needed for the runways. The noise of the bulldozer and the electric saw gave way to that of concrete mixers and lorries, while down in the valley the Aparoans began to pick up the threads of their lives again. New thatched houses began to take the place of the old ones and the bigger boats that now came into the harbour brought replacement supplies, building materials and furniture.

A new clinic was one of the first buildings to be erected, and soon the house was clear of patients and Tansy could have her room to herself again. She welcomed the return of privacy and went often to sit for hours at the window, gazing out at where the knoll of trees had once stood. Just sitting—and remembering. The long, slowly passing days had done nothing to heal the ache in her heart, the terrible, agonising frustration of longing that filled her every time she thought of Blake. And she thought of him so much; only by concentrating on her work until she was exhausted could she shut out the memories. She felt like a woman whose fiancé had been killed—having had the promise of shared happiness but having tasted only enough of its delights to leave her longing eternally for more.

Over the next few weeks she became thin and wan, her usual vitality completely gone. Often her father would

177

come upon her staring abstractedly out to sea, she would become aware of him and give a bright, artificial smile for his sake and start to talk animatedly, only to lapse into silence again after a few minutes.

Everything seemed altered; even Ruari seemed different as he took on more of his father's work and responsibilities. One day Tansy was having a drink with him on the veranda when he casually announced that he had decided to get married.

She looked at him in surprise. 'This seems very sudden. Who's the lucky girl?'

He looked down at his glass. 'Lait. She'll soon settle down once we're married.'

'Yes, I'm sure she will,' Tansy had agreed faintly, and from then on she had seen little of Ruari. There had been a feast—the food supplied by the government—to celebrate the marriage, and after that she had seldom gone to Tupuhoe's house unless her father was with her.

He was looking forward with anticipation to his new life in Sydney, writing and receiving endless letters from his Evelyn, whose photo now adorned the piano in the sitting-room. Nearly four weeks after Blake had left the island the plane that now brought the mail regularly instead of it coming once a month on the trading schooner brought a pile of letters for them. Eagerly Tansy sorted through them; there was a thick wad for her father, but nothing for her. Dejectedly she put them down; she didn't really know why she searched, it was a forlorn, lost hope. She knew that Blake had been too bitterly hurt for his pride to let him get in touch with her. If she wanted him she would have to be the one to make the first move, but she longed desperately for some word from him, to know how he was, if he was well, if he ever thought of her.

Her father came in and picked up the bundle of letters

from where she had dropped them on the table. There were two letters from Evelyn confirming the final arrangements for their wedding and these he read out to her.

'I've been trying to arrange for that young Australian doctor to take over for a week or so while you come to Sydney with me for the wedding,' he told her. He pushed aside a couple of circulars and picked up a large, type-written envelope. 'Ah, this looks as if it could be the Medical Board giving a yea or nay.' He opened the letter and began to read, drawing in his breath sharply as he did so. But Tansy didn't stay to hear the verdict; she had wandered out into the garden and went to sit on a stone bench beneath a trailing hedge of mauve bougainvillaea. Abstractedly she plucked a flower and closed her eyes as she lifted it to her face to breathe in its heady scent. It brought a vivid remembrance of the few short hours she had spent in Blake's arms. Her body ached for the touch of his hands, her mouth for the warmth of his lips on hers.

'Of all the infernal impudence! Tansy, just look at this!'

Her reverie was shattered by her father's angry command and she opened her eyes to see him holding the letter out for her to read. Quickly she took it, wondering what on earth could have made him so annoyed, but he was so irate that he hardly gave her time to see that it was from the Medical Board before he began to tell her himself.

'Do you see what they have the temerity, the nerve, to write to us? They accept my resignation all right, but they refuse your application for the post! Say they've decided to appoint a Commissioner to take over the running of Aparoa during this difficult period and that he

insists on appointing his own medical staff! Have you
ever heard such damned nonsense in your life? As if anyone could be more suitable for the job than you! And I
shall write and tell them so, too. These damn men sit at
their office desks and think they know everything. Just
wait till I tell them what I think of them, I'll ...' David
Harland broke off as he saw the look of shattered bewilderment on his daughter's face as she stared at the
letter in her hand. 'There must be some mistake, Tansy.
Now don't you worry, I'll get them on the radio and ...'

'They don't want me,' Tansy said slowly, in little more
than a whisper. 'I gave up so much. I let him go and now
they're not going to let me stay here.' She looked dazedly
up at him, gave a small, uncertain gasp and then began to
shake with hysterical laughter, her breath choking between laughs and tears of despair. Immediately her father
took her in his arms and she clung to him unashamedly
as the hysteria gave way to great, racking sobs that
seemed to fill her chest to bursting, as though she would
choke on her own unhappiness.

'Tansy, my dear child!' There was consternation in her
father's voice as he tried to comfort her. 'What did you
mean, let him go? What is it, my dear?'

In a small, broken voice she told him of her love for
Blake and of the two other loyalties, to himself and to
Aparoa, that had combined to make her send him away.

Appalled, he listened to her with mounting distress.
'Why on earth didn't you tell me? Something could have
been done, something would have been arranged.'

'What? What could you possibly have done except give
up all thoughts of Evelyn so that I was free to go with
Blake?' She shook her head and then picked up the letter
from where it had fallen to the ground. 'And now it
seems as if they don't want either of us,' she said bitterly.

'They don't even have the courtesy to tell us the name of the new Commissioner, only that he's been appointed and will be arriving as soon as possible to take up his duties. But, Daddy, how will the islanders manage with a stranger over them, somebody who probably won't even speak their language?' There was deep concern in her voice as she asked the question.

Her father stood up and began to pace up and down the lush green lawn. 'You know, thinking about that,' he replied at length, 'it occurs to me that perhaps we're wrong. Perhaps the government are doing the right thing in sending strangers here, after all. Life on the island has changed completely now, whether we like it or not, and the islanders will have to learn to adapt, be taught a new way of life that will fit in and around the fuel base. Learn new trades so that they can be employed at the base and gain independence that way. But we represent the old life, my dear. If we stay here we might hold them back, our longing for the old Aparoa might be greater than theirs, for to them there was nothing wonderful about it; only to us, who have seen other ways of life, was it a precious thing to be fought for at all costs.'

He turned to draw her to her feet and put an arm round her shoulders. 'Do you know where your young man is now?' Tansy nodded and he went on, 'Then you must write to him straight away while the plane is still here.'

Her eyes widened as she looked at him. 'But what can I possibly say?'

He patted her shoulder reassuringly. 'You'll find the words.'

But her father's easy assumption was far from reality. She had spent two hard, frustrating hours trying to compose a letter to Blake; in one effort being stilted and cold, in another pouring out all the aching desire and longing that she felt for him. But every time they ended in the waste-paper basket. This letter mattered so much; she was afraid to say too much, afraid to say too little. If only she could have picked up a telephone and spoken to him! She knew that at the sound of his voice everything would have come right, but to have to try to put it on paper! In the end she had run out of time and the letter she finally sent was a short, rather formal one that merely told him that her plans had changed and she wouldn't be staying on Aparoa after all. She ended by saying that she would probably go to Sydney with her father and try to get a job there.

As she gave the envelope to the pilot of the mail-plane she almost snatched it back; she hadn't said anything that she really wanted to say, hadn't told him she loved him, hadn't begged him to come to her just as fast as he could. But it was too late; already the pilot had stuffed it into the mail bag and was climbing up to the flight deck.

That had been over three weeks ago. And since then she had heard—nothing! There had been no cable that Blake was coming, no message over the radio, no letter by the mail-plane. At first she could reassure herself that it was too soon, that he couldn't have received it, but she had asked for the letter to be sent on by air-mail and knew that he should have received it within a few days. Then she convinced herself that he must have been away and it had to be forwarded on to him, but as the days dragged on with still no word her thoughts had begun to be tortured by doubts. Did he still want her? Or had he had time while he was away from her to regret his impetuosity? Maybe it was the beauty of Aparoa that had thrown an enchantment over him, and now that he had returned to a more sophisticated world, he would look back on those few hours of love as an interlude of summer madness when the magic of the island had awakened him to a brief passion that he was now glad to have escaped?

Eagerly one morning she cycled to the base as soon as the mail plane flew in, not even trusting one of the little native boys to collect the letters for her, but again this morning there was no envelope for her in Blake's firm, thick writing. Her face set, she politely thanked the nice man at the base who sorted the mail and looked at her so curiously, then turned her bicycle round to ride slowly, unseeingly down to the clinic. There was the usual line of people and Tansy listened to all their complaints, patiently and gently treating them, advising them as she had always done, but there was a dullness in her face, a depth of unhappiness in her eyes that held them back from asking any questions; instead they brought little gifts to try to please her and make her smile. One of them even brought her a carved model aeroplane that he had copied from the aircraft like the one that even now came in to land, and which had already become so commonplace that the islanders no longer ran out to watch every time one flew over.

At length the last patient had gone, clutching his bottle of medicine, and Tansy slumped back into her chair, feeling physically exhausted. Reluctantly she realised that she couldn't go on like this; hardly eating, lying awake half the night and then only sleeping fitfully, waking with jangling nerves at the slightest sound. She didn't want to resort to sleeping pills, but her father was becoming increasingly concerned about her and she didn't want to worry him further. Automatically she straightened her hair in front of the mirror, the dark shadows under her eyes accentuating the thinness of her face. The blouse and skirt she was wearing were also too large for her now. She had never worn her sarong since the earthquake; those carefree days when she was just one of the island girls had gone for ever.

Tansy came out of the clinic into the sunlight and then stopped abruptly, her heart palpitating in her chest. Blake was leaning nonchalantly against a treetrunk, his arms folded, just as he had stood so long ago on the day that he had arrested her and put her in the prison! She blinked hard and then looked again—it was all right, it wasn't a mirage, he was very real. He straightened up when he saw her but made no move to come to meet her. He was in uniform, but a different one from that he wore previously. This time he had trousers instead of shorts, and in place of the beret he wore a peaked hat that shaded his eyes so that she couldn't see them. Slowly, quiveringly, she walked towards him.

He looked down at her enigmatically, his expression unreadable, deliberately waiting for her to make the first move.

'H-hallo, Blake,' she managed, her eyes desperately searching his face for some sign of emotion, but he continued to look at her stonily.

'You sent for me.' His tone was cold, almost impersonal.

'Oh, but I ...' she said swiftly, but then broke off as she saw the sudden spark of fire in his grey eyes.

'Did you or didn't you?' he asked forcefully.

Tansy looked down, her heart beating painfully. 'Yes,' she breathed, and slowly raised her eyes to look at him appealingly.

'Get in the jeep.' He turned and walked towards the vehicle, climbing in without waiting for her, letting her walk round and get in by herself, not looking at her. As soon as she was beside him he started the engine and drove along the coastal road for a couple of miles until they came to a track leading to a small, jungle-flanked cove. He pulled up on the edge of the beach and took off his hat to run a hand through his dark hair before tossing the cap on to the back seat. Getting out of the jeep, he walked towards the water's edge.

Tansy watched him for a few moments, unable to recognise this person as the man who had made love to her so passionately only a few weeks ago. He was so forbidding, a tall, implacable stranger of whom she almost felt afraid. Hesitatingly she got out and followed his footprints across the white sand. He turned and watched her walk towards him, his eyes appraising her so that she stopped uncertainly a few feet away from him.

Her lips quivered. 'Blake, I . . .' She tried hard to control herself. She wanted so much for him to take her in his arms, but he deliberately refrained from touching her.

His voice suddenly savage, he said, 'That was one hell of a letter!'

Miserably she lowered her head, her hands clasped tightly together. 'I'm sorry. There was so much I wanted to say, but I . . .' She looked at him unhappily, his face was still set and cold. Desperately she said, 'Blake, I know how much I hurt you and I . . .'

'No!' he interrupted harshly. 'You'll never know how much!' He swung away from her and walked a little further down the beach to lean against a high rock, his hands in his pockets, gazing out to sea. 'So you're not going to take over your father's job?' he asked at length.

'No. The—the government have appointed a Commissioner to take control of the islands. He wants to choose his own medical staff.'

'I see.' He turned round to face her. 'So now that you can't stay on Aparoa, you've sent for me.' With a slight sneer in his voice he went on remorselessly, 'I don't like being second best, Tansy. Especially to a damn island!'

She stared at him despairingly; how could she break down this iron barrier that he had erected about himself, how convince him that she needed him so much? There was only one way that she knew. Taking a deep breath she said as firmly as her quivering heart would allow, 'I love you, Blake.'

Eagerly she scanned his face for some answering emotion, but beyond a slight tightening of his jawline there was none. 'You said that before,' he said in cruelly scathing tones. 'It didn't seem to mean much to you then. Why should it now?'

Flinching as if he had struck her, Tansy turned away, unable to bear his coldness any longer.

'Stay where you are!' he ordered harshly before she had taken more than three steps. Unwillingly she obeyed, but didn't turn round to face him.

Blake came to stand behind her and she could feel his breath stirring her hair. 'I've been given a fresh posting. It's in a rather primitive part of the world, miles away from anywhere, and I shall be there for at least two years. It might be better if you took a job in Australia—perhaps I'll look you up when I get leave.'

Tansy turned round then, her eyes large and staring as she looked into his. She wanted to beg him to stop hurting her like this, to throw herself into his arms, but she could only say woodenly, 'Can't you—take me with you?'

Inscrutably he looked down at her. 'Yes, I can take you. But if I do, it will be on my terms.'

'What—terms?'

'That you come to me without reservations. Follow me

wherever I'm sent.' There was urgency in his voice now, and for the first time a hint of the emotions that he held so rigidly in check showed in his face. 'Well, will you come with me?'

Almost shaking with relief, Tansy found that she couldn't speak, could only nod her head. Tentatively she held out a hand towards him, but he made no move to take it.

'Are you sure?' he asked relentlessly. 'This time there'll be no backing out, Tansy.'

She let her hand drop to her side and bit her lip. He demanded no less than complete and utter submission. Then she raised her head to look steadily into his dark eyes. 'Yes, I'm sure,' she managed. 'If—if you still want me.'

'Want you?' His voice had changed now, become husky and ragged. He reached out and put his hands on her shoulders. Tansy began to tremble beneath his touch, the touch that she had yearned for for so long. Slowly he drew her towards him. 'Yes, I still want you,' he murmured, and with infinite slowness, almost as though he were afraid to do so, he bent his head to seek her lips with his. For a few seconds his mouth was gentle against her own, but then he pulled her roughly against him, imprisoning her hands against his chest, his lips ravaging hers compulsively, forcing them apart. He kissed her with the fervour of a man who has been marooned on a desert island for years, and held her so tightly that he bruised her flesh. Tansy returned his kiss ardently, her only thought the aching desire that he aroused in her, that and the necessity to convince him of her need for him.

At length he raised his head and loosened his hold a little, but Tansy stood on tiptoe to throw her arms round his neck and cling to him.

'Oh, dear God, Tansy,' he muttered huskily into her

neck, 'don't ever walk out on me again. It's been hell ...'

'Blake, Oh, my darling, I won't. I promise I won't.'
Tears ran down her cheeks and she put up a hand to
brush them away.

He held her a little away from him and looked at her;
at her thinness and the dark shadows round her eyes.
'What the hell have you been doing to yourself?' he said
roughly.

'Missing you,' she said softly. 'Oh, Blake, I missed you
so much!'

Sweeping her back into his arms, he held her close, just
holding her, letting her feel the warmth and comfort of
his body hard and firm against her own, until she had
stopped shaking and could smile up at him as she blinked
away the tears.

'Dearest,' he murmured as he bent to kiss away a tear-
drop that still clung to her cheek. 'We'll go to Tahiti. We
can be married in Papeete and have some time there for
a honeymoon before I—before I take up my new posting.
We'll have at least a ...' he broke off as he saw that
Tansy was looking at him in happy wonderment.

'You—you mean we're going to get married?'

Blake looked at her in some astonishment. 'But surely
you realised that ...? Tansy, did you really think I would
make you anything less than my wife?' he demanded incredulously.

'I didn't know. You never said—just as you never said
that you ...' She stopped and looked away from him.

'That I loved you?' There was a frown between his
brows as he cupped her face in his hands. 'Darling, I've
told you a hundred times; every time I looked at you,
touched you, I was telling you how I felt about you. I
want you, I need you, by God I do. If that isn't love ...'

'Oh, Blake, if only you'd told me before! It would

have made that letter so much easier to write. By then I was completely unsure of myself; afraid that you wouldn't want me any more, especially after you got back to England and saw all the girls there.'

He laughed softly and pulled her head down into his shoulder. 'The girls in London don't walk around in those tantalising sarongs.' Then he added teasingly, 'Although there were one or two girls that I quite ... Ouch!' He broke off with an exclamation as Tansy bit his ear. 'You little minx!' He made a grab for her, but she slipped agilely from his grasp and ran away from him across the beach. He let her cover a dozen yards before he caught her and bore her down beneath him on to the soft sand. Then it was a long, long time before either of them felt the need for any speech other than passionate endearments.

It was only when Tansy lay quietly pillowed in his arms that she asked, almost idly, 'Where is your new posting? How soon do you have to go there?'

Lazily Blake sat up and then turned to her with a rueful, somewhat boyish grin. 'I'm afraid I rather deceived you about that. You see, I wanted to make sure you were fully committed to me before I told you.'

Tansy pushed herself up to kneel beside him, her hair dishevelled, her blouse undone, but her eyes shining with a new radiance. 'Told me? But I don't understand. Don't you have a new posting, after all?'

'Yes.' He took her hand and raised it to his lips to kiss her fingers, his eyes, with a roguish glint in them, never leaving her face. 'You see, darling, I knew that I couldn't live without you, so I decided that if I couldn't have you without Aparoa, then I'd have to do something about it. So I moved heaven and earth and finally convinced the powers that be into accepting that what these islands needed was a resident officer to get the place back on its feet. That part wasn't too difficult, but then I had to persuade them that I was the right man for the job.'

He went to go on, but Tansy's fingers had closed compulsively over his. 'You—you mean that you're the new Commissioner?'

'Well, I couldn't let some other chap come over here and let you doctor him, now could I?'

'Oh, Blake! Blake!' With a cry of pure joy, Tansy flung herself upon him and knocked him off balance as she threw her arms round his neck to hug him. She kissed him exuberantly before raising her head to smile down at him as he lay with a smug, contented expression on his face.

He opened one eye. 'I don't remember telling you to stop,' he complained.

Tansy laughed at him, but then, her face serious, she said, 'You'll never know how much this means to me, Blake. Thank you. Thank you so much.'

He smiled. 'Well, you see, there was one lesson that I neglected to teach you when we were waging that private war of ours; a good soldier always knows when to surrender.' And he drew her gently down beside him.